BEVERLY HILLS MAASAI

ALSO BY ERIC WALTERS

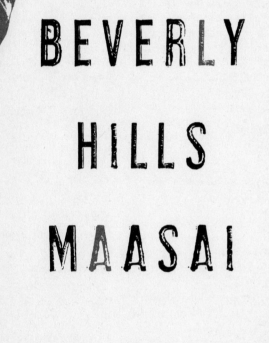

BEVERLY
HILLS
MAASAI

ERIC WALTERS

DOUBLEDAY CANADA

Copyright © 2010 Eric Walters

All rights reserved. The use of any part of this publication,
reproduced, transmitted in any form or by any means electronic,
mechanical, photocopying, recording or otherwise, or stored in a
retrieval system without the prior written consent of the publisher—
or in the case of photocopying or other reprographic copying,
license from the Canadian Copyright Licensing agency—is an
infringement of the copyright law.

Doubleday Canada and colophon are registered trademarks

Library and Archives of Canada Cataloguing in Publication
has been applied for

ISBN: 978-0-385-66903-0

This book is a work of fiction. Names, characters, places and
incidents are products of the author's imagination or are used
fictitiously. Any resemblance to actual events or locales or persons,
living or dead, is entirely coincidental.

Book design: Jennifer Lum
Printed and bound in the USA

Published in Canada by Doubleday Canada,
a division of Random House of Canada Limited

Visit Random House of Canada Limited's
website: www.randomhouse.ca

10 9 8 7 6 5 4 3 2 1

BEVERLY HILLS MAASAI

CHAPTER ONE

The phone rang again, startling me so much that the nail polish brush jerked off my toenail and onto the white separator holding my toes apart. If any polish spilled on my new duvet, someone was going to have to pay!

"You're awfully jumpy, Alexandria," Olivia said, lounging at the end of my king-size bed.

"I'm not jumpy. I just don't like the sound of ringing phones."

The phone kept on ringing.

"Carmella!" I screamed.

"Just ignore it," Olivia told me.

"I *have* been ignoring it," I said.

This was the third time it had rung in the last ten minutes, and it was really starting to get on my nerves. Where was Carmella? It wasn't like the call was going to be for me—anybody who knew me called on my cell—and it certainly wasn't my job to be answering the home phone.

Four . . . five . . . six . . . seven rings. You'd think the person on the other end would have figured out that nobody was going to answer. Couldn't they just leave a message and move on? Were they deliberately trying to get on my nerves? And where *was* Carmella? She was supposed to get the phone. That *was* part of *her* job.

"Carmella!" I screamed at the top of my lungs.

"Either she's out or she's ignoring you," Olivia said. "We've had a couple of maids like that. Some of them pretended that they didn't understand English."

"Some of them probably didn't understand English," I argued.

The phone stopped ringing, and I let out a sigh of relief.

I took the brush and dipped it into the bottle of polish, careful to take just enough. The way to get great nails—aside from using the very best polish money could buy—was to apply many, many thin coats. Some people either didn't know that or didn't have the patience, but I knew how important it was to have the details just right.

The secret to a great look is in the details. Any fool with a little bit of money can buy the right clothes or designer accessories—and there certainly are enough fools in L.A. with money to do that—but there's an art to putting them together the right way, to making the look work for you. It's easy to tell the pretenders from the contenders—although I was no mere contender . . . more like the champ!

"My mother says that good help is almost impossible to get," Olivia said. "Do you have any idea how many maids we've gone through in the past year?"

"You're on your seventh," I said.

"Yes . . . that's right," Olivia said. She looked surprised.

"Your mother told my mother," I explained.

"We even caught one drinking on the job!" Olivia exclaimed.

"Really?" I tried to sound shocked, but if I'd worked for Olivia's family I might have started drinking too.

"She was going right into the cabinet and drinking my father's private stock."

"Oh, really?" I said. "Does that remind you of anyone you know?"

"That was ages ago," she protested. "And I was only fifteen."

"As opposed to the old woman of sixteen that you are now?" I asked.

"Sixteen is *much* older than fifteen," she argued. "You'd have to agree with that."

Actually, I did agree. "Touché."

"Besides, it was *my* father's alcohol I was drinking," she added. "It wasn't like I was stealing from somebody else . . . but you'd know all about *that*."

So she was fighting back! I tried not to react. There was no way I was going to let her know she was getting to me.

"We all make mistakes," I said casually. "Some of us learn from them."

"Not necessarily the first time," she said, and chuckled.

Again, I didn't react, although I really had the urge to see how her face would look with nail polish all over it.

I'd been caught shoplifting once. And before that I'd dented a girl's car to pay her back for her catty comments about my at-the-time boyfriend. They were mistakes, and I'd paid for them. But really, I wouldn't change anything that happened to me as a result, even if I could. The whole thing worked out for the best. There was no doubt about that. None whatsoever.

I didn't answer. I just kept my complete focus on my toenails.

"You've had Carmella for years, haven't you?" Olivia said.

"She's been with us forever. I think we hired her when I was, like, three."

"Thirteen years is a long time. You know, that's when you have to be careful," Olivia said.

"Careful?"

"Yes. Once they earn your trust, that's when they start to slack off, or worse yet, things get up and walk away."

"You've had maids who stole from you?" I asked.

"My mother had her favourite necklace, a very expensive necklace, go missing."

"And the maid took it?"

"That's why my father fired her."

"And did you call the police? Was she charged?"

"My father said it was too hard to prove anything. He said Manuela would just deny it and it would be her word against ours."

"That's too bad," I said.

"My father said we could have made a claim through our insurance company."

"Could have?" I asked.

"Well . . ."

Olivia looked sheepish, and I knew there was more to this story, something she didn't want to say. I might have let her off the hook if she hadn't brought up *my* mistakes first.

"Well, what?" I asked.

"Funny thing," she said, although her expression wasn't very amused. "It turns out it really wasn't stolen. It had fallen behind the dresser . . . We found it a week or so after she was canned."

"After you found the necklace, did you rehire Manuela?" I asked.

"Of course not!" Olivia protested. "That would have been too embarrassing. Besides, it's not like it's hard to find another maid."

"Or even six more," I said.

The phone started ringing again. This time it set off my little Pomeranian, Sprout, who had been sleeping peacefully in his doggy bed but now was barking his yappy head off. As if the phone's incessant ringing wasn't bad enough by itself without the dog turning it into a duet.

"Carmella!" I screamed.

"At least *our* maids all answered the phone," Olivia chuckled.

I'd had enough of the ringing—and of Olivia. I got to my feet.

"What are you doing?" she yelled. "You'll ruin your nails!"

"I'll take that chance."

I hobbled forward, trying to walk on my heels, with the toe separators keeping my toes apart and up in the air.

"Carmella!" I screamed again. "The phone!"

That was a pretty stupid thing to yell because obviously if she'd heard it ringing she would have known it was the phone.

I went into my parents'—my *mother's*—bedroom. There was a phone on her night table. Delicately I picked it up, trying not to smudge my fingernails.

"Yeah?" I snarled.

There was no answer. Had I stomped all this way for a hang-up? No, there was no dial tone, so there had to be somebody on the other end. Was it one of those stupid telemarketer calls where they make you wait for them? So rude!

"Hello? Is anybody there?" I demanded.

"Hello?"

It was a male voice with a foreign accent. Was it Spanish? If this call was actually for Carmella I'd be so angry—

"Hello," he said again. "Could I speak to Alexandria . . . Alexandria . . . I think the last name starts with an 'H.'"

"This *is* Alexandria. Alexandria *Hyatt*."

Stupid telemarketer. If he was going to harass people he should at least know their full names. I should just hang up on him right—

"Alexandria, I did not recognize your voice."

And just why did he think he should? It *had* to be some stupid telemarketer—we got them all the time. At least some of them were slick enough to get your attention, but this guy was simply *hopeless*.

"I thought that you were not home, or that I had the incorrect telephone number," he said. "I called many times and no one answered."

"That was *you* calling?" Now I was *really* mad.

"It was me."

"When we didn't answer the first three times, didn't you understand that maybe there was nobody home?" I demanded.

"That is why I called back again and again."

Strange, there was something about his voice that did sound familiar.

"So why are you calling?" I asked. I just wanted to get to his pitch so I could blow him off.

"You told me to call."

"What?"

"You said to call you. You gave me your telephone number."

"Who is this?"

"It is Nebala."

I was so shocked I almost dropped the telephone, grabbing it, smudging a nail as I caught it. "Nebala— *my* Nebala—from Africa?"

He laughed, and I recognized the laugh even more than I had the voice. "Do you have many other Nebalas in your California?"

"Of course not! I'm just so shocked, so surprised, so happy to hear your voice!"

"And *your* voice is very pleasant to listen to also," he said.

I pictured Nebala in my head, in full Maasai costume—red blanket and dress, wearing sandals, a bow over his shoulder and a *konga* club under his blanket—standing there somewhere in Kenya with the phone in one hand and his spear in the other.

"I just can't believe I'm talking to you!" I exclaimed.

"The elders in my village still think of phones as being magic, too."

"I don't mean the phone part. I mean talking to *you*. It's unbelievable that we're talking, that you called me!"

"Very believable. You gave me your telephone number and I just pushed the buttons. Very easy."

"But it must be costing you `a fortune to make this call."

Long distance from Kenya would be incredibly expensive, and it wasn't like he had a lot of money— like anybody in his village had a lot of money.

"Not too much, I do not think. I put in two of those silver coins. I think that is not much money."

Silver coins? I tried to remember what the different Kenyan coins looked like, but it wasn't coming.

"I wish to ask something of you," Nebala said.

"Of course. What do you want to know?"

"Do you remember that when you left Kenya, you said that someday you would welcome me to come to your country, to your land?"

"Of course I remember!" I exclaimed. "That would be wonderful! I told my parents about everything in Kenya, but I especially told them all about you and Ruth! My mother and father said they'd be thrilled to meet you someday!"

"I would be honoured to meet them. They must be very wise people."

"And I could show you around L.A. the way you showed me around Kenya."

"That is so kind."

"I owe you," I said. "I don't know what would have happened to me if you hadn't been there for me in Kenya." Because being "there for me" actually meant saving me from a herd of elephants—something not a lot of my friends could have helped with.

"You are strong without my help. You are so strong you could even be a Maasai."

I laughed. "I don't think anybody would ever mistake me for a Maasai. I think I sort of have the wrong skin colour."

"You have the heart of a Maasai."

I knew what a compliment he was giving me. "Thanks, but I don't think I could kill a lion."

He laughed. "Of course not. You are a *woman*. Even Maasai women do not kill lions."

"It would be wonderful if you *could* come to California. But it's awfully far from Africa!"

I didn't mention how expensive the plane fare would be—way more than he could ever afford.

"It is very far," Nebala said. "Even your country is very big, and far from one place to another. It is a long way from New York to the other side in California," he said.

"It would be a long walk."

"It is a long airplane ride," he said. "But a Maasai could walk from one side to the other of a country even as big as America."

"I know, I know, because Maasai can walk without stopping," I said.

"Never needing to stop from sunrise to sunset."

It was something they prided themselves on. I could picture him with that long, bouncy stride. Given enough time, I was sure he *could* walk from New York to L.A., or even from Africa to L.A. if there wasn't an ocean in the way. I imagined him moving along the interstate, and the shocked looks from the drivers of passing SUVs and cars and transport trucks.

"To walk across your country would take more than one hundred days," he said.

"I don't know," I said. I guessed he must have been looking at a map. "I'm not sure if anybody has ever done that before, walked across the country."

"A Maasai could walk that distance."

I wasn't about to argue with that. They were pretty stubborn and determined people.

"And if you did come here, you know I would insist that you stay at our house," I said. "We have a big house with lots of extra rooms."

"I was hoping you would allow that."

"That would be wonderful, if you did come someday." That sounded like I was blowing him off. "I'd like it if you could come someday *soon*."

"Yes," he said. "Soon, very soon. Alexandria, I am at the airport."

"In Nairobi?" I exclaimed.

"LAX. I am in Los Angeles."

That time I did drop the phone.

CHAPTER TWO

The tires squealed as I turned the corner.

"Alexandria, slow down!" Olivia insisted.

"Are you afraid of a little speed?"

"It's not the speed, it's the wind. It's absolutely *ruining* my hair!" she exclaimed. "Could you either slow down or put up the top?"

"I haven't got time for either."

Olivia made a cross little puffing sound and then scrunched down in the seat until she was so low that I didn't think she could even see over the dashboard. If she had been driving she would have been looking through the steering wheel like some sort of really ancient senior citizen. It was strange how the older people got the bigger their cars got. Around here, though, the senior citizens all had chauffeurs to do their driving for them.

"This is so . . . so bizarre," Olivia said.

"What's so bizarre about going to the airport to pick somebody up?"

"This isn't *somebody*. This is some guy from Africa you hardly even know."

"Wrong! I know him very well."

"How well could you know him? You were only in Africa, like, a month."

It was three weeks, actually, so she was close on that one. I didn't expect her to understand any of the rest.

"And I can't believe that you're going to let him stay at your house."

"Where else would he stay?"

"There are hotels, you know."

I tried to imagine Nebala at the Beverly Hills Hotel—dining at the Polo Lounge, lying by the pool as starlets and models strutted past in their bikinis and high heels. I laughed out loud.

"This isn't funny!" she screamed. "You told me how scary these Maasai are! You told me they are the most dangerous warriors in all of Africa!"

"They are dangerous . . . if you're a lion. I'll be fine. *We'll* be fine."

Of course Olivia knew I had been in Africa—and why. I'd been caught shoplifting, and the judge had sentenced me to go to Kenya to build schools as part of what they called a "diversion program." But she really had *no* idea what it was like. Nobody who had never been there would ever understand how . . . *different* it was, how special the people were, how it changed who you were, your very soul.

"And I can't believe that you haven't even asked your mother about any of this. What will you do if she says that he can't stay at your house?" Olivia asked.

I looked over at her, slowly shook my head, and then we both broke into laughter.

"Well, she *could* say no," Olivia chided.

"Not likely. I can't even remember the last time she said no to anything I asked. You know what I'm talking about."

"Ha! Yeah, I just play my mother against my father and I can get almost anything I want, too." She paused. "But with your father not living with you . . . well . . ."

"He may not live with us, but he's only a phone call away."

"I hear you," she answered.

Really, all I usually had to do to get my mother to cave was *threaten* to call my dad. I knew it would still work, but I hadn't gone there in a long time. It just made me feel guilty to play them that way.

Of course my mother almost never said no to anything, anyway. Partly it was because she really wanted to make me happy, but partly it was because she was so wrapped up in her own life—or trying to find a life—that she didn't much notice what was going on in mine.

We rolled along the road leading into LAX. There were lots of cars heading in, and I had to slow down. We passed the coloured columns that lined the entrance. There were twenty or thirty of them, some as high as 120 feet. I loved the way they looked, not just from the ground but from the air. If you flew in from the right direction you could see them as your plane came in for a landing, especially at night. They were like "welcome home" signs.

"Where are we meeting him?" Olivia asked.

"In front of the terminal."

"Which terminal?"

"He didn't know which one, so I told him to just go out front and stand by the road. Keep your eyes open for him."

"There are hundreds and hundreds of people standing by the road waiting to be picked up, and I don't even know what he looks like."

"Think about it, Olivia. He's going to be wearing a bright red blanket, and I would imagine he's the only Maasai warrior who came into LAX today . . . or any other day."

"Sorry. Duh!"

Traffic slowed as cars and cabs swerved and stopped to pick up passengers and their luggage. It was hard to believe just how crowded it was, but then again, this was one of the busiest airports in the world.

"I told him to stand by the circle road."

"Why didn't you ask him which terminal?"

"He didn't know the terminals," I said.

"But there are nine of them. This could be difficult."

"So we'll just keep driving past, one by one, until we see him."

"Did he even tell you why he was here?" Olivia asked.

"I didn't ask. I thought it was best to get down here as soon as possible. He's got to be feeling a little lost."

"That makes this all so *ironic*," Olivia said.

"Ironic" was a word she used a lot, but she almost always used it wrong.

"Well, don't *you* think it's ironic?" she asked.

"Okay, I'll bite. What's ironic?"

"In Africa he was your guide and he protected you from danger, and now you're rushing here because you think you need to protect him."

I guess that *was* kind of ironic. "Not protect him. It's just that it's all going to seem pretty strange, and he's alone and—"

"There he is!" Olivia screamed.

"Where?"

"There, over there," she said, pointing up ahead.

Instantly I saw him—bright red against a sea of black and white and bland. I put my foot on the brake and swerved into the curb lane, cutting off a taxi. It blared its horn at me in protest. I raised one hand so the cab driver could see that I was giving him the universal symbol of response to honking. What a jerk.

I pulled over to the curb and squealed to a stop right in front of him. I jumped out of the car and ran around the front.

"Here I am!" I screamed, waving my arms in the air. "It's so good to—" I skidded to a stop just a few feet away as I was about to wrap my arms around him. It wasn't Nebala. It was a stranger—a strange Maasai warrior!

He stood there, shield in hand, staring at me. He looked older than Nebala. His expression was fierce, and I stumbled backwards a step.

"I'm so sorry . . . I thought you were somebody else," I stammered.

He didn't react. His expression remained fierce and frightening.

Olivia appeared at my shoulder, just slightly behind me.

"You mean this isn't him?" she asked.

I shook my head vigorously, and Olivia started to laugh. I turned to her, surprised and confused by her reaction.

"Apparently, there *is* more than one Maasai warrior coming into LAX today," she explained. "Ask him if he knows Nebala."

"Just because they're both Maasai doesn't mean that—"

"Nebala?" He stepped forward then, and I had to fight the urge to retreat.

"Nebala?" he asked again.

I nodded my head. "Yes, yes. Nebala."

He started talking, a stream of excited Swahili.

"What is he saying?" Olivia asked.

"I have no idea."

"But I thought you spoke Swahili."

"I speak a *little* Swahili, and only if it's slow Swahili. I can ask for some food or say thank you or hello, but I don't really know how to speak it," I protested.

"Well, try to say something to him," Olivia said.

"Sure . . . okay . . . I'll try." But what? I didn't think asking him where the washroom was located would do. But what about asking where Nebala was? I could do that, couldn't I? I struggled to find those words in my brain. I wanted to make sure I could pull out the right words, because the last time I'd made a mistake in Swahili I'd threatened to kill somebody by accident.

"Um . . . um . . . *wapi* Nebala?"

"Nebala!" he yelled, and I started and Olivia screamed.

He reached out and grabbed me by the arm and started to drag me toward him. I dug my heels in and struggled. Maybe he knew Nebala and didn't like him— or maybe he really was bringing me to him—but I couldn't just leave my car or it would be towed away. I tried to back away, but he had me firmly in his grip.

And then I saw him, through the glass doors, inside the terminal. Nebala was walking toward us, a shield in one hand and a large cloth bag in the other. He was far away, but he stood out so clearly—the bright red, the shield, and that long, bouncy stride eating up the distance between us.

"There he is!" I screamed and pointed.

The mystery Maasai let go of my arm then and nodded his head enthusiastically.

"*Naam, naam!*" he yelled, and he too pointed at the terminal.

"What does that mean?" Olivia demanded.

"It means 'Yes, yes!' It's him. It's Nebala."

"Samuel . . . *Naam, naam*, Samuel," he said.

"What? I don't understand . . . What do you mean?"

"Maybe he means that's somebody named Samuel," Olivia volunteered.

I huffed. "Yes, there's a Maasai named Samuel, and I'm sure there's another one named Taylor, and Cody."

"Samuel," he repeated.

"There, he's saying it again!" Olivia protested.

"Of course he's saying it, but we don't know what that word means in Swahili. He's just saying something about Nebala and—" I stopped myself mid-sentence.

The figure was now close enough for me to realize that it *wasn't* Nebala. It was *another* unknown Maasai warrior. He was taller and thinner and much, much younger. Nebala was grown up—he'd already been to college in Nairobi—but this guy couldn't have been much older than us. He quickly came toward us wearing the traditional red blanket, like the scary guy, but with a gigantic smile plastered across his face.

I quickly scanned the surroundings. Was there a third Maasai somewhere?—Nebala? Or were there many, many more? Were we being invaded by the Maasai? Had the whole airport gone Maasai mad? Was there a gigantic Maasai convention in town? Maybe that was why Nebala was here. I couldn't see any more, though—I couldn't see Nebala anywhere.

What I did notice was that we were now at the very centre of a large crowd of people who were staring at us. Dozens and dozens of travellers had put down their luggage and were watching us. Some of them had taken out cameras and were clicking pictures, and cars were stopping so people could gawk at us—well, really, at the Maasai.

The second Maasai came right up to us and dropped his bag to the sidewalk.

"Samuel," he said, and touched his hand to his chest.

"I told you that was his name!" Olivia trumpeted.

"We still don't know that!" I protested.

The first one tapped his hand against his chest. "Koyati!" he said proudly.

"And that one's Koyati," Olivia said. She pointed at herself. "*O-liv-i-a*," she said slowly and loudly. "I am *Olivia*."

"O-liv-i-a," they both repeated, nodding their heads in acknowledgment.

"And this," Olivia said, placing a hand on my shoulder, "is Al-ex-an-dri-"

"Alexandria!" the young man screamed. "Alexandria!"

They both got all happy, and the young man—was his name really Samuel?—started jumping up and down like a very big, very excited three-year-old.

"They must know you!" Olivia exclaimed.

"I don't know them," I said.

What I did know was that the crowd surrounding us was getting bigger and bigger, and the space between us and them was getting smaller as they pressed in on us from all sides.

"We need to find Nebala," I said. "*Ne-ba-la*," I said again, this time much more slowly and much, much louder, the way Olivia had.

A figure pushed through the edge of the crowd. There stood Nebala, at last!

CHAPTER THREE

I rushed over and threw my arms around Nebala. I felt myself on the verge of tears, but I bit down on the inside of my cheek to drive them away. Crying seemed so . . . so babyish. Tears, I knew, would not be respected by a Maasai warrior. He wouldn't cry if he was impaled on a spear.

"It's so good to see you," I said softly.

He pushed me an arm's length away and looked at me intensely, like he was studying me. "Good to see you, Alexandria, too. Very good." He nodded his head.

I turned and pointed to the other two warriors, who were standing with Olivia. "I thought they were you."

"Them?" Nebala sounded shocked. "They do not look anything like me!" He paused. "I am *much* more *beautiful* than either of them."

He started laughing, and I suddenly felt relieved.

"Come, meet my friends."

"Okay, so those guys really are with you, right?"

"Of course. Did you think three Maasai warriors all appeared at once by some chance?"

"Well, I had kind of figured that it was too strange to be a coincidence."

"No coincidence. They are with me."

"Just the three of you . . . right?" I asked, very nervously. One Maasai warrior was going to be hard enough to explain to my mother. Three was going to *very* difficult. A whole tribe would be *impossible*.

He pointed at himself. "One." Then at the two of them. "Two, three." He held up three fingers. "Yes, *tatu* . . . three."

Okay, three was a lot, but it could have been worse. And I didn't think my mother would be three times as freaked out as she would have been by one.

"This is my friend Olivia," I said.

"I'm so pleased to meet you," she said as they shook hands. "Alexandria has told me so much about you! About how you were her guard, and how you saved her from a herd of charging elephants and everything!"

"Maybe I saved the elephants from Alexandria," he said.

"What?" Olivia looked more confused than usual.

"He's just joking, Olivia."

"Oh, okay," she said, and giggled nervously.

"These are members of my village, of my tribe," said Nebala. "This is Koyati."

Koyati stepped forward. His expression was frozen and fierce.

"He is of my age group. He has killed three lions and is *very* brave."

"I thought all Maasai were brave," I said.

"All Maasai *are* brave," Nebala confirmed. "But Koyati is without fear. His bravery is known to all Maasai."

"I'm happy to meet you," I said.

He bowed his head slightly but neither moved nor changed his expression. He looked scary.

"He understands some English but speaks almost none."

"That should make for some interesting conversations," I said.

"And this is Samuel."

"I *told* you that was his name," Olivia said—again.

He stepped forward the same way Koyati had, but rather than just standing stoically and staring blankly, he smiled until his whole face lit up. Even his eyes were smiling at us.

"He is younger. His group has just come of age. He killed his first lion just two years ago. And he has learned some English."

"*Jambo*, Samuel," I said, greeting him in Swahili.

He reached out and grabbed my hand and began pumping my arm up and down.

"Hello, *dude*," Samuel said.

Both Olivia and I broke into laughter, and for a split second I thought we might have hurt his feelings, until he started laughing as well.

"Perhaps I should have mentioned that there were three of us," Nebala said. "Does your house have room for three?"

"Her house has room for thirty-three!" Olivia beamed.

"There's space," I said. "I'm glad to have your friends as well. I was just a little surprised, that's all. I'm sure that—" I saw a parking control officer standing by my car, and it looked as though he was writing a ticket.

"Hey!" I screamed as I ran over to my car.

The parking officer looked up at me and scowled. He didn't look any friendlier than Koyati.

"I'm right here!" I protested. "You don't have to write me a ticket!"

"It's a little late for that," he said. He ripped the ticket out of the book and handed it to me.

"But I was just over there picking up some—"

"The sign says no stopping, no parking." He pointed at one of the gigantic signs that were on every pillar in both English and Spanish. "Can't you read?" he demanded.

"Of course I can read. Probably better than you!" I snapped.

"Well, guess what? I can read what I just wrote on that ticket."

"And that's probably the most complicated thing you've ever read," I said sarcastically.

"No, the most complicated thing would be the summons when I have a car towed away! You move it now or I'm going to have it—"

He stopped mid-sentence and I realized why.

On all three sides we were hemmed in by Nebala and Koyati and Samuel. They stood, holding their shields, forming a wall that surrounded us.

"Is this girl your wife?" Nebala demanded.

"What?" the parking officer asked.

"This girl you are talking to, is she your wife?" he repeated.

"No, of course not," he scoffed.

"Is she your daughter?"

"My daughter? Look at her!" The parking control officer was black, and you couldn't get much whiter than me.

"Is she even of your tribe?" Nebala asked.

"I don't . . . I don't have a . . . a tribe," the man stammered.

"If she was of your family or your tribe you could perhaps use such a tone of anger and disrespect," Nebala said. "But she is not, so you have no right to talk to her this way. You need to apologize."

The three pressed in close until he was hemmed in against the side of my car with no escape. Now all three wore the same fierce expressions, and he looked terrified.

"Back off!" he yelled. "Or . . . or . . . I'll call for backup!"

They pushed in even closer. This was definitely going to end badly. I'd learned in Kenya that the Maasai didn't think it was murder if you killed somebody who *wasn't* a Maasai. I had to do something right away, or the only part of Los Angeles they'd see would be a jail cell.

I shoved back in between Samuel and Nebala and got right into the ticket officer's face.

"I demand that you call somebody!" I trumpeted. "Get on that radio right now and call your supervisor so I can complain about how you have treated our guests! Do you have any idea who these men are?"

He shook his head vigorously, his eyes still wide with fear.

"This is *King* Nebala's son. He is a prince." So maybe the Maasai wouldn't use that term. Whatever. What else would you call a king's son?

Nebala's shoulders straightened and all three moved back a half step.

"He is royalty, and you have treated him with inexcusable disrespect."

I reached down for his radio and plucked it off his belt.

"Call right now and get your supervisor. You might find that this is the last ticket you'll ever write."

"I'm really, really sorry," he sputtered. "Really sorry . . . I didn't know. I didn't mean anything . . . I'm sorry, really."

I turned to Nebala. "Is that apology sufficient for you?"

"He needs to apologize to you, Alexandria, for his harsh words and tone."

"I'm sorry to her, too!" he exclaimed. "I didn't mean anything! Here, let me take that." He reached out and took the ticket back from me and ripped it in two, and then in four and eight, and dropped the pieces to the pavement.

I handed him back his radio.

"Thank you," I said. "Now is it good?" I asked Nebala.

He didn't answer at first. He looked as though he was studying the situation, studying the man. Nebala finally placed a hand on the man's shoulder. "Friend. All is good."

The man grabbed Nebala's hand and began pumping it up and down. He reached out and did the same with the other two, and then with me and finally with Olivia.

"You just sit here as long as you need," he said. "Do you have to get luggage?"

"Oh, yeah, luggage," I said. "Where is your luggage?"

"Samuel has all our belongings," Nebala said, motioning to the canvas bag that was on the ground beside him.

"Talk about travelling light," Olivia said. "My makeup bag is bigger than that."

I looked at the crowd that was surrounding us. It had continued to get bigger and bigger. There had to be hundreds of gawking people, all watching, all waiting for something to happen. And then, through the crowd, I saw two policemen moving our way. I wasn't going to count on them being as agreeable— or gullible—as the parking control officer.

"Okay, everybody into the car!" I exclaimed. "Quickly!"

I picked up the bag—it was heavier than I'd guessed—and tossed it into the back seat. It landed with a metallic clatter.

"Olivia up front, and the three of you in the back!"

Olivia opened the door, and I grabbed Samuel and practically pushed him into the back. The other two followed. It wasn't a very big back seat, and the three of them, their bag, and their shields were all squashed together. Olivia climbed in to the passenger seat, and I circled the car, jumped in, and started it up.

"Nice meeting you!" the parking control officer yelled out.

Samuel stood up and waved to him. "Good night, *dude!*"

I squealed away from the curb and Samuel almost toppled out of the car. I looked back through the rear-view mirror. The parking guy continued to wave goodbye. He was now flanked by the two officers. I'd got away without a second to spare.

CHAPTER FOUR

I kept one eye on the road and the other on the rear-view mirror as we swerved away from the terminal. I was relieved that my backwards glances continued to reveal no police cars following behind. What they did reveal was the reality that there were three Maasai warriors, clutching their shields, in the back seat of my Mustang convertible. Somehow Samuel, who had got in first, had managed to get into the middle. His face, his wide smile, filled the rear-view mirror.

I turned the mirror, angling it so I could see Nebala.

"Nebala, this is all a pretty big surprise," I said, yelling loud enough to be heard over the roar of the wind.

"No surprise. You invited me, so I came."

"I mean I was surprised by you being here now."

"Now is the time."

I wasn't sure what that even meant. Was it like Maasai philosophy?

"I figured you might have called to tell me you were coming."

"I did call . . . That is how you knew to come to the airport to get us," he said.

"I didn't mean call me from the airport. I meant why didn't you call me from Nairobi and let me know you were on your way?"

"There was not time. I just found out. We had to come now."

"Why now?"

"It is the time. It is when it will happen."

"When *what* will happen?" I questioned.

"The run . . . when the run happens."

"What run? What are you talking about?"

Nebala pulled out a piece of paper. He reached over the seat to offer it to me.

"I'm driving! Olivia, can you take it?"

Olivia grabbed the crumpled piece of paper and straightened it out.

"*A cut above the rest,*" she read out. "*You are invited to the inaugural Beverly Hills Marathon on Sunday, February 25.*" Olivia turned around in her seat. "You've come all this way to watch the marathon?"

"Not watch. Run. We are here to *run* the marathon."

"I had no idea you were a runner," I said. "How long have you been training?"

"We are Maasai," he replied simply.

"What does that mean?" Olivia asked.

"They spend their whole lives running," I explained.

"Without stopping. Never rest," Nebala added.

"I guess if you're running a marathon you can't stop or—" I caught a glimpse of something in the mirror. I took a quick glance backwards. Samuel was standing up, his arms extended into the air as if he were flying!

"You have to make him sit down!" I yelled.

Nebala said something to him in Swahili, and Samuel answered but didn't sit down.

"He says he is too happy to sit. Too excited. He has never been in a car before."

"You're joking, right?" Olivia asked.

"No."

"But you live hundreds of miles from Nairobi, so how did you get to the airport if you didn't come in a car?"

"Walked."

"You walked . . . hundreds of miles?" Olivia said.

"Close to three hundred."

"Wow! I don't even like it when I have to park too far from the entrance to the mall," she said. "Thank goodness for valet parking."

"What does that mean . . . 'valet parking'?" Nebala asked.

"It's nothing," I said. "Just something lazy people use so they don't have to walk."

"Hey! Hey!" Olivia protested. "You use valet parking. I've been with you!"

"I didn't say I wasn't lazy."

Olivia turned around in the seat to face Nebala. "I just can't believe that you walked hundreds of miles."

"That's nothing. We are——"

"Maasai," I said, cutting him off. "We know, we know."

"I guess that's great training for a marathon," Olivia added.

I noticed the people in the car beside us gaping and laughing and pointing. I'd forgotten about Samuel. He was still standing. In fact he seemed to be standing even taller, as if he was on his tippy-toes. His blanket was blowing and flowing behind him like a cape. If he'd had a big "S" on his shield he could have been "SuperMaasai."

I looked all around. Once again we were the centre of attention. All we needed now was a police car to pull us over. I was sure that none of the guys had their seat-belts on——they wouldn't have known what they were.

"Samuel *has* to sit!" I yelled. "Tell him it's dangerous."

Nebala said something to Samuel, who said something back and then started to laugh. What he didn't do was sit down.

"What did you say to him?"

"He said he is not afraid of danger because he is——"

"I know, I know." This was getting old fast. "It's just that if I have to stop suddenly he'll fly right out of the car!"

Nebala translated again and Samuel answered. More laughter, but he continued to stand.

"What? What did he say?"

"I told him you could make him fly like a bird, and he wanted you to show him because he has always wanted to be a bird."

That wasn't the plan. But I knew one way to make him sit.

"I'm surprised that he doesn't listen to you. I thought that because you're King Nebala's son, a very respected Maasai, he would listen to you . . . especially since he is practically just a boy."

Nebala barked out something, and Samuel dropped down to the seat as if he'd been shot. He sat there meekly, looking down at his feet. Maybe he wasn't smiling anymore, but I was.

CHAPTER FIVE

We slowed as we came up to the entrance to my house. I pushed a button on the remote and the gate glided open. We passed through and onto the grounds.

There was a burst of Swahili from the back seat and I turned slightly. Samuel was pointing at the gates as they closed behind us. I hadn't even considered what they might think. If Samuel had never been in a car before, he'd certainly never seen an automatic gate.

"It works with this," I said, holding up the remote.

"I explained," Nebala said. "There are gates like that in Nairobi for big houses and hotels."

"Yeah, of course."

Nairobi was a big city, I remembered—it had as many people as Los Angeles.

We drove up the driveway past the rows of sprinklers watering the lawns. I didn't want to go right up to the house—I wanted to tell my mother about our guests before she saw them. I pulled up and parked.

"This is your house?" Nebala asked.

Olivia laughed. "This is their *garage*."

"Garage?"

"Where they keep their cars."

Nebala pointed to the guest house. "There. Is that your house?"

"That's *your* house while you're here," I said.

"And your house?"

"That's the big one you saw as we drove up," Olivia explained.

"That is where your tribe all lives?" Nebala asked.

"Just my family."

"I did not know you had such a big family," Nebala said. "How many brothers and sisters?"

"Just me."

He looked shocked. "None? No others?"

I shook my head. "I'm the only child."

"In such a big house?"

"It's not that big," Olivia said.

It was certainly bigger than *her* house, I almost snapped—but I kept my mouth closed. She wasn't trying to be snotty; it was just a fact. Compared to some of the monster mansions in the neighbourhood my house was almost modest. Everybody living here had money, but some people had *real* money. There was a big difference between rich and *super*-rich. We were somewhere in the middle.

"A house so big for only a few," Nebala said. "It would be so . . . so . . . lonely."

"It's okay. I have friends, and of course Carmella and Carlos are always here."

"They are friends?"

Olivia scoffed. "They're the maid and the gardener."

"What is this . . . *gardener*?" Nebala asked.

"It's somebody who cares for the grounds."

"The ground?" he asked, still looking confused.

"Not the *ground*, the *grounds*. Plants and flowers and the grass and trees—things growing outside the house."

"Ah, yes," Nebala said. "This man, this *gardener*, he must be very wise."

"Um . . . I've never really thought about that," I admitted.

"Do you know about such things?" Nebala asked. "About the earth and how things grow?"

"Of course not!" I protested. I didn't have time for this discussion right now. "Olivia, could you settle them in while I talk to my mother?"

"For sure," she replied.

Samuel jumped out of the car, over the trunk, as the rest of us climbed out through the two doors. Nebala carried their one bag.

"The door to the guest house should be open," I said. "I'll be down as soon as I can."

They started off, and I couldn't help watching. Olivia, all blonde and tanned and perfectly coiffed, wearing her Gucci sunglasses, led the three red-robed Maasai, shields in hand, across the perfectly manicured grounds. It was a bizarre sight, and I certainly understood why so many people had stared.

I'd made the decision to put them in the guest

house and not the main house while we were coming up the driveway. The guest house had three bedrooms, a kitchen, a full bathroom, and a simply *wonderful* view of the pool and gardens.

It also had the advantage that it would keep them a little bit farther away from my mother. This was going to be more than just a surprise for her. It would be bordering on shock. I knew she wasn't going to say no to their staying with us, but I was still a little nervous about how she might react. With my mother there could be a wide range of responses—everything from just smiling and agreeing to something approaching a full-fledged anxiety attack, complete with having to breathe into a paper bag to stop hyperventilating, taking a little blue pill, and having to lie down. If it went that way, I was going to end up feeling pretty guilty.

Although, come to think about it, I couldn't remember her having one of those anxiety attacks for quite a while. Either she wasn't having them anymore or she was having them when I wasn't around.

For a split second I played around with the idea of not telling her at all. She was out a lot, and when she was home she hardly ever went to the guest house . . . No, I couldn't do that. If she did wander out and discover them by accident she'd have a *heart* attack instead of an anxiety attack. I'd have to tell her, but I'd have to tell her gently.

I opened the front door. The house was completely quiet. And big and sterile and empty. I felt a tinge of loneliness. It really was a big house for just two of us. In Nebala's village there would have been lots of little huts, with five or six or ten people in each one—each about a fifth of the size of our foyer—and the huts would all be clustered together, in a little circle, with a big open space in the middle for the cattle to be safe at night.

"Hello!" I yelled out.

My voice echoing off the walls was the only response I got. Maybe my mother wasn't even home yet. I walked through the foyer toward her "studio." Well, that's what she was calling it now. It used to be my father's office—the place where he spent more of his time than any other place in whole house. Now that he wasn't living here anymore he certainly didn't need an office. That was one of the reasons my mother had given for choosing that room—that and the fact that it had a lovely view of the garden. I thought there might be more to it than that.

Changing the office into a studio had involved a *massive* renovation. The room had been stripped down completely, with the floors and walls and even the ceiling ripped out. There was nothing left that gave even a hint of my father's having been there. It was as if the whole room had been cleansed of his presence. I guess my mother needed that. But I missed the office—the familiar furniture, the smell of my father's cigars and cologne.

As I got closer I heard some kind of dreamy New Age music. That had to be my mother. Carmella's music was loud and Latino.

The door was open and I peeked in. While the rest of the house was clean and organized, this room was nothing more than a big jumble. It was filled with paintings and statues and pots and vases and quilts. Some were finished, but many had simply been abandoned. There was a potter's wheel, two easels, boxes of paints, a loom, and mounds of fabric and wool. All the equipment was the best money could buy, bought brand new and discarded even before the warranties could lapse. They were like the orphans of my mother's previous hobbies, ventures, and plans.

She started each new project with such enthusiasm— at first, it would be all she could talk about. She'd spend hours and hours, excitedly occupied, fascinated and focused. Then, time after time, all of that would be replaced by apathy, disappointment, despair, and finally . . . nothing.

I knew what she was doing. Since the divorce she'd lost her way, lost her role. She was no longer a wife, and that was about all she seemed to know how to be. She used to say that she and my father were kind of a team—she would take care of everything at home, including me, so he could devote himself full time to his business. And she would arrange dinner parties with clients, organize fundraisers for worthy causes, and do all the other social things that helped give him status in this status-crazy city. Now, without that part to play, she was trying to "find herself." But all she'd found out so far was that she wasn't a painter, or a sculptor, or a quilter, or a potter. She needed to find out who she was.

My greatest fear was that she was going to start dating again . . . dating younger guys. Beverly Hills really was becoming Cougar Town. I couldn't imagine anything worse than what happened to a friend of mine—running into her mother while she was out clubbing, bumping into her at the bar. How incredibly embarrassing! And to make it worse, they were dressed almost identically! I figured there should seriously be a law against people over thirty wearing stilettos and spandex.

I was startled out of my thoughts when something moved, catching my eye. It was my mother, down on the floor in her black exercise clothing, stretching on her little exercise mat. She was in the enthusiastic stage of one of her latest passions—yoga.

"Hey, Mom," I said.

She inhaled deeply and then released her position and slowly rose to standing. I had to admit she was doing it pretty well, sort of gracefully, like a cat or a ballet dancer.

"Hello, my darling," she said. "Would you like to join me?"

"Thanks, but not right now," I replied.

She raised her hands above her head, touching her palms together, then raised one foot until it rested against the thigh of her other leg.

"Standing Tree," she said.

"What?"

"This position is called Standing Tree."

That name at least made sense. There were so many terms she'd thrown at me over the past month—the Cobra, the Bridge, the Lotus, and of course my favourite, Downward-facing Dog. My dog, Sprout, was *very* good at that last position. On occasion my friends and I had done "hot yoga." It was like regular yoga but in a room only slightly less hot than an oven. Talk about feeling the burn! It was good exercise, but I really didn't like working up that much of a sweat, nor did I have time to learn all those silly names for positions. Just tell me to lie down, touch my palms to the floor, whatever.

But at least I could appreciate yoga . . . well, I appreciated all the clothing associated with yoga. There were some wonderful outfits by some of my favourite designers. Of course, just as with stilettos and spandex, I figured there should be a "best before" age limit on yoga clothing.

My mother said that yoga was making her feel younger. I don't know how many times over the years I'd heard her say that "forty is the new thirty," or "fifty is the new forty." By that logic, dead must be the new eighty.

"This is *so* relaxing," she said.

She did sound relaxed. Calm. That might be helpful right now.

"You really should try this," she urged me.

"That's okay. I just wanted to ask you something," I said.

"You could ask while assuming this position." She lowered her leg and came over to me. "Here, let me show you."

I knew there was no point in arguing. Soon this latest craze would pass and we could file yoga under painting in the "past hobby" category. Although this little obsession had been going on for a while. That and computers. What a strange combination: something from ancient times and computers. And of course she had the most up-to-date, modern, expensive computer that money could buy—that my *father's* money could buy. She was taking a course. It was almost amusing to hear her talking about the Internet as if it had just been invented.

I tried to mimic her yoga position. She helped move my leg up and shifted my hands a little so they were in the right position.

"Now isn't that restful?" she asked.

"Sitting is restful. Lying down is even more restful."

"Just hold the position, and you'll see."

I found myself working hard to maintain my balance and not topple over.

"You wanted to ask me a question?" she said.

"Yeah, right." I wanted to word this just right. "I was wondering if you'd mind if I had some friends over."

"You know your friends are always welcome in our home," she said. Her voice was very calm, and I noticed her eyes were closed.

"I was actually hoping they could stay with us for a few days."

"How many of your friends will be with us?" she asked without looking at me, eyes closed, lost in her Standing Tree.

"Three friends."

"Are their parents out of town?"

"Yes, they are." That wasn't a lie. Africa was definitely out of town.

"And for how many days, exactly?"

I thought about the date on the flyer. The marathon was in four days, so it wouldn't be much more than that. "Four, possibly five days."

"It will certainly make for a busy house."

I lost my balance and stumbled as I put my foot back down to stop myself from tumbling over.

"It's not as easy as it looks," she said.

"I never thought it looked that easy."

My mother exhaled deeply and lowered her foot to the ground. She looked at me and tilted her head slightly to one side.

"You look very tense," my mother said. "Nervous . . . as if there's something that needs to be released."

I felt a little unnerved. Of course there was something else. I just wasn't used to my mother noticing.

"Well, my friends . . . they're not really from around here," I said.

"Oh, are they from the Valley?"

"Well, you could say that. They're sort of from the *Rift* Valley."

"The Rift Valley? Isn't that in Africa?" she asked.

"Yes, it is." I paused. "And that's where my friends are from."

"Africa?"

I nodded my head. "They're already here. How about if you come out and meet them?"

CHAPTER SIX

"I hope you haven't insulted our guests by having them stay in the pool house instead of the main house," my mother said.

It was encouraging to hear her call them *our* guests.

"I think they'll be fine out here. It *is* a guest house, really," I told her as we circled by the pool.

"Do you think so? It's just that it's not especially nice," she said apologetically.

"They normally live in huts made of mud and cow dung," I explained.

"Oh, my. I guess this will be fine, then."

She knew there were three of them. She knew they were from Africa. I just hadn't quite found a way to tell her that they were three Maasai warriors. I guess that would become pretty obvious, pretty soon. She'd taken the first two pieces of news remarkably well. Maybe she'd take the third the same way. Maybe not. It might be better, I thought, if she heard it from me instead of finding it out for herself.

I understood now that giving somebody only *part* of the truth was pretty much the same as lying. Our family therapist had talked us through that. We'd been seeing her—my mother, my father, and I—ever since I'd returned from Africa. Sometimes it felt kind of pointless. But not always. Sometimes it was actually really helpful.

Before my trip to Kenya my parents had separated, then divorced, but even though my father didn't live with us we'd worked things out so that I still spent a lot of time with him. It was only after I'd returned, though—after my life had been changed by that experience—that we'd all agreed to meet for therapy. My parents weren't getting back together, but they were still both my parents, and we all had to live on the same planet, so it was best that we learned to get along. The biggest lesson I'd learned from therapy was that the truth can be painful, but it's always better than the alternatives.

I grabbed my mother by the arm to stop her. I had to tell her. I just wasn't sure what to say. Maybe a delay would give me time to think.

"Shouldn't you get changed before you meet our guests?" I suggested.

"I'm very comfortable in my yoga clothing."

"How about a shower? You were really working up a sweat in there."

"I think of it as more of a glow."

"I just want you to make the best possible first impression," I argued.

"So do I, and not rushing right out to meet them would leave the impression that I'm not thrilled to have them here. We can't have that, now, can we?"

I shrugged. She was making a pretty good point.

"I can't wait to meet your friends." She started walking again.

I reached out and grabbed her a second time. I put myself between her and the guest house.

"Actually, only one of them is really my friend. You know . . . from before," I said.

"Is it Ruth?" she asked.

Ruth was the Maasai girl I'd become good friends with when I was in Kenya. I wished it were Ruth. I missed our time together, our conversations.

"Not Ruth, but from the same tribe as—"

"Oh, my goodness!" my mother gasped, her eyes widening in surprise, and all of the colour drained from her face.

I hardly needed to turn around because I knew what I was going to see. Slowly I looked over my shoulder. Olivia and the three Maasai had come out of the guest house.

"They . . . they . . . they're . . . "

"They're our guests."

"But they're . . . they're . . . "

"Maasai. They're Maasai, like Ruth."

"But why are they here?"

I was impressed. She'd recovered enough to ask a full question.

"They're going to run in the Beverly Hills Marathon."

"And . . . and they're going to stay *here*?"

"They're my friends. I want you to meet them."

I took her by the hand and led her toward our guests. Koyati and Samuel had both squatted down at the edge of the pool and were talking so excitedly that they didn't even seem to notice us. Nebala did. He offered a big, friendly smile in greeting.

"You are Alexandria's mother?" he asked.

"Yes . . . I'm Rachel Hyatt."

He turned to the other two and barked out something in Swahili. They both quickly got to their feet and flanked him, facing us.

"We have been asked to pass on the gratitude of our tribe for what you have done," Nebala said. "It is a great thing."

"It's nothing . . . a few days in the guest house."

He shook his head. "Not for now. For before. For the clinic."

"Oh, the clinic!"

When I'd returned from Africa I'd told my parents about how the people of the village had to travel long distances to get medical treatment, and how people were dying because of the distance. My parents decided to donate money to set up a clinic—money they'd set aside to buy me a very expensive car for my sixteenth birthday. I'd suggested they buy me a Mustang instead, so the villagers got their clinic.

Nebala and Koyati exchanged words and then Koyati stepped forward. My mother stumbled back slightly—his expression was so serious and so fierce. Didn't this guy ever smile?

Koyati said something to my mother and then reached out and grabbed her hand in both of his. She looked terrified and tried desperately to pull her hand away, but he held her in place.

"He says his family owes you a great debt. Because of your gift, the life of one of his sons was spared."

"It was nothing," my mother said.

"No, no," Nebala said. "It was everything. It was his *oldest* son."

"I'm . . . I'm so glad . . . glad to hear that," my mother sputtered. "What I meant was that the money wasn't that much. It wasn't much at all."

Koyati said something else. He was still holding my mother's hand in his.

"He says that he has to offer his thanks to your husband as well."

"He's not here right now," I blurted out before my mother could answer.

"He doesn't live here anymore," my mother said icily.

Nebala looked confused.

"My parents are separated."

He still looked confused.

"He's gone."

"He is dead?" Nebala asked.

"Not dead!"

"I wish," my mother mumbled under her breath.

I shot her a dirty look.

"Sorry," she added. "That wasn't fair or kind."

"My parents are divorced," I said, trying to explain it further. "They are no longer married."

He still looked confused. Maybe Maasai didn't get divorced. Maybe he didn't even know what it meant.

"When a husband and wife can't get along anymore, when they fight too much, they decide to live in different houses. My father lives in a different house."

Nebala nodded his head and then explained things to the other two. They became involved in an excited discussion, with Koyati being the most vocal.

Nebala turned to us. "Koyati said that if your mother would like it, he would take her as a wife."

My mother giggled. "Thank him so much for his offer, but I think I've had enough of men for now."

Nebala nodded and then translated, and they talked some more.

He turned to us again. "He said he understands, but there is always room if you change your mind. He said that you would like his other wives."

"His *wives*? How many wives does he have?" my mother questioned.

"Only two. You would be his third."

"Is it okay in your tribe to have a lot of wives?" I asked.

"My father has seven," Nebala said.

"Seven! That's unbelievable."

"He told me that seven is too many," Nebala said. "I think that's why he spends so much time with his cattle, to get some quiet."

I couldn't help laughing. That was why my father had spent so much time in his office. Apparently, some things didn't change from one culture to another.

"Alexandria tells me you're here in Los Angeles to run in the Beverly Hills Marathon," my mother said.

Nebala shook his head. "We did not come to run."

I was startled. "But . . . but . . . you told me that's why you came—to run in the marathon."

"Yes, but we did not come just to run. We came to win."

"Winning isn't everything," my mother said.

Now it was Nebala's turn to look confused. My mother obviously didn't understand the Maasai. Losing was a concept they did not take lightly.

"Oh, my heavens!" my mother gasped.

I turned around. Samuel and Koyati were squatting down on the deck and, with cupped hands, were drinking from the swimming pool.

"I can get them some water if they want!" my mother exclaimed.

"Is that water not for drinking? Is it for your animals?" Nebala asked.

"No, of course not!" my mother exclaimed. "That's our pool . . . for swimming. That's pool water. I can get them bottled water, sparkling, if they want something to drink."

Nebala nodded his head. "Yes, water would be good."

"Where are my manners?" my mother said. "Let me offer you all something to eat. There's a recipe I've been dying to try out."

"You're going to cook?" I gasped. I didn't know if I was more shocked or scared.

She laughed. "Of course not. It's a recipe I want Carmella to make."

That certainly made more sense.

"After such a long trip, you three must be famished," my mother said.

"What is 'famished'?" Nebala asked. "What does that mean?"

"Hungry," I explained.

"Yes. Hungry, yes."

"Did you have a meal on the plane?" my mother asked.

"No. Not on the plane. We ate before we got on the plane."

"You haven't eaten since New York?" I asked.

He shook his head. "Kenya. We ate in Nairobi before we got on the plane."

"But . . . but . . . that was yesterday."

"No. Two days ago."

"You haven't eaten in two days?" I was shocked.

He shrugged. "Two days is not long."

That might explain why they were drinking from the pool.

"We'll get you something to drink and eat immediately," my mother said. "You must be starving!"

"It would take many more than two days to starve," he said. "Much longer."

I knew that wasn't an innocent statement. Where he came from, "starving to death" wasn't just an expression; it was something that could really happen.

"All of you come to the house right now, and while supper is being prepared we'll serve some appetizers," my mother said. "And of course, water."

CHAPTER SEVEN

I motioned for the Maasai to sit down. They all seemed very unsure about what I was asking.

"Please," I said. I pulled out my chair and sat, and then they did the same, settling in at the dining-room table.

I had to hand it to my mother: she had gone all out on the table. The tablecloth was white linen—Italian linen—and she'd set out the bone china, crystal glasses, our best silver, all arranged around a beautiful floral centrepiece. The table looked perfect. It would have impressed the Queen of England. Unfortunately, the Queen wasn't sitting at the table.

"What would our guests like to drink?" my mother asked.

Nobody answered.

"We have tea, coffee, juice, wine, sparkling water, and—"

"Water," Nebala said. "We would like water, please."

My mother picked up a little bell and rang it. Carmella poked her head into the room.

"Could we please have water for everybody," my mother said.

Carmella nodded and disappeared into the kitchen. When she came back out, she filled all the crystal glasses from a bottle of sparkling water.

"So you're all runners," my mother said.

"Yes," Nebala answered.

"I myself am into yoga."

"What is yoga?" Nebala asked.

She looked surprised that he didn't know, but pleased that she'd have the opportunity to tell him. She had become, over the past few months, the Yoga Queen.

"It's an ancient Hindu philosophy that allows the integration of body, mind, and spirit," she began.

Nebala looked completely lost.

"It is a way for a person to seek inner contentment through the—"

"It's exercise," I said, cutting her off.

"It's so much more than that," my mother said with a laugh. "It's more like a form of meditation."

"That's not going to help," I said. I turned to Nebala. "Do you know what meditation is?"

He shook his head.

"It's a way to create a kind of inner peace." She paused. "Actually, I have friends who run, and they tell me that running can produce that same sense of peace. Do you find running peaceful?"

Nebala didn't know what to answer to that question either. It was obvious, even to my mother, that this wasn't clearing up his confusion.

"It gives them time to think," she continued. "What do you think about when you run?"

"I think about when I can stop running and walk again," he answered.

I laughed.

"Or if I can catch what I run after . . . or get away from what is chasing me," he continued.

I laughed again. There was a twinkle in his eyes, so I knew he was just joking.

"Surely you must get something more out of running?" she questioned.

"It's just how they get around," I said, trying to explain. "It's not like they all have cars or can hop on to the subway. Maasai run because it gets them where they have to go."

"But there has to be more to it than that," my mother protested.

"I don't think so," I said, shaking my head. "They just run to move, either to get something or somewhere, or to get away from something or somewhere."

"But if that's the only reason, why are they here now to run in the marathon?"

I hadn't thought about that. That was a good question.

"If it's simply running to get around, they wouldn't have come halfway across the world to run in Beverly Hills," my mother said. "There has to be more."

"Nebala," I said, turning to him. "Why *did* you come to Beverly Hills to run in the marathon?"

"To win," he said.

"Yes, yes, I know you want to win, but why did you come all this way, to Beverly Hills, to run in this particular marathon?"

"To win," he repeated.

"But . . . but . . . why didn't you just stay in Kenya and run?"

He laughed. "There is no money to run in Kenya. Here is money."

"Money?"

He reached into his pouch and pulled out that yellowed flyer announcing the marathon. He placed it in front of me and tapped his finger against the advertisement. There, at the bottom, was a list of the prizes for the event.

"Oh, wow!" I gasped.

"What is it?" my mother asked.

"The person who finishes first gets $250,000!"

"I had no idea," my mother said.

"Second place is worth $150,000, third gets $100,000, and fourth place receives $75,000." I turned to Nebala. "You're running for the money?"

He nodded.

That didn't make any sense. Maasai didn't collect money, or cars, or houses. All that mattered were cows. The more cows a warrior owned, the richer he was. Wait . . . maybe that was it.

"I understand! If you win, then you can buy more cows, right?"

He shook his head.

"Then what are you going to use the money for?"

He picked up his glass and held it out toward me. "Water."

"Sure, we can just ask Carmella for another bottle."

"No, no, the prize money is for water."

"You're going to buy . . . water?"

"We will dig a well so that we have water for everybody."

"I'm confused," Olivia said. "You mean, you *don't* have water now?"

"The rains did not come this season—again. The river has dried up. There is little water . . . not enough. What water we have is not good."

"And that's why you came here to compete in the marathon. That's why you need the money," I said. Now it all made sense.

"Yes. People are sick . . . cattle are dying."

"Have you had cattle die?" I asked.

"I have no cattle," Nebala said, his words barely audible.

"Of course you have cattle . . . you even told me how many cattle you have."

"Had," he said sadly.

"*All* your cattle have died?" I gasped. "That's awful!"

"All my cattle have been sold." Nebala gestured to Koyati and Samuel. "We all sold our cattle. That is how we got money to fly here."

"I just can't believe you'd do that," I said.

I knew that to a Maasai, his cattle were second in

importance only to his family. I couldn't imagine a Maasai selling his cattle.

"There was no choice. Without water *all* the cattle will die." He paused. "People will die." He paused again. "And that is why we *must* win the marathon."

CHAPTER EIGHT

I shifted my weight in bed and turned over onto my other side. I'd drifted off a couple of times but hadn't really been able to get to sleep. Too many thoughts, too many surprises. In my wildest dreams I had never imagined that Nebala—and two other Maasai— would be staying in my guest house. This was all beyond belief.

I sat up in bed and tried punching my pillows. If I could get them in just the right positions maybe I could settle in and get to sleep. My father always joked that I was like "The Princess and the Pea" and needed my bed to be just perfect.

I snuggled back into the pillows and kicked at the covers until my feet were free. I had to get to sleep, which meant I had to forget about Nebala and go to my "happy place." Not that I wasn't happy about

Nebala visiting . . . I was. It was just that it was all so strange and unexpected. And my thoughts drifted back, of course, to my summer in Kenya.

Who would have thought that a shoplifting charge, combined with an angry judge, would have landed me in Kenya with a program to build schools? And if it hadn't been for that, I never would have met Ruth— "my Maasai sister," I called her—and I would never have learned to look at the world in an entirely different way, and . . . This wasn't helping me get me to sleep.

I rolled over again to face the window. The breeze felt soft and cool and . . . Where was that breeze coming from? I looked over. My window was open. I hadn't left my window open. I *never* left my window open. I opened my eyes as wide as I could to try to capture whatever light was coming in through the window—through the *open* window. Trying not to move much, or more important to be seen to move, I slowly turned my head so I could look around the room. It was dark. I could see only shadows and— Was there somebody standing in the corner? I stifled a gasp and felt a scream rise in my throat. Wait . . . it couldn't be a person. My imagination was running away with me.

Our house had an elaborate alarm system. We'd always had an alarm—who didn't?—but after my father moved out my mother upgraded to a system that most banks would have been envied. Since then, she'd been much, much more relaxed. Still, she always armed the alarm when she went to bed. I was safer sleeping in my own bedroom than in a bank vault.

So what if my window was open? I probably hadn't latched it properly and the wind had just blown it open . . . although the wind did seem pretty gentle. But so what? It wasn't like anybody could get in through my window anyway. I was on the second floor—really almost as high as the third floor because of the way the ground below was landscaped and dropped off—and there was no way anybody could climb up the side of the house. It was a straight drop.

I didn't like heights, and I didn't like looking straight down from my window. If you ever fell it would be one big drop to the ground. You'd probably break your neck, unless some of the shrubs below cushioned your fall.

There was a tree not far from my window, but it wasn't close enough to climb up to my room. There was no way. I knew that for a fact. The security experts who'd installed the alarm system upgrade had also done a full security audit of the property. Based on that, they'd removed some of the shrubs, installed motion-sensor lights, and trimmed branches from the trees that were too close to the house.

Carlos had been *so* angry. He treated the trees and shrubs as if they were members of his family, and he just couldn't believe that these security guys had hacked away the branches. He called them a bunch of butchers. I think he would have taken a chainsaw to *them* if he could have got away with it.

Now you'd have to be a leopard to leap from that tree to my window, and this wasn't Africa. There was nothing more dangerous here than a chihuahua. But that shadow in the corner was a lot bigger than a chihuahua, and it certainly didn't look like a leopard. Not like a leopard . . . but it did look like a man. Paranoia was back for an encore.

I tried to focus my eyes on the shadow. If I stared harder maybe I could see better. This was stupid. Why didn't I just turn on my bedside lamp? Then this whole thing, my imagination running wild, would dissolve in the light.

Unless it really *was* a man standing in the corner of my room . . . standing there watching me sleep . . . waiting for the right moment to—The shadow moved!

Slowly I moved my hand from under the covers, inching it closer to the light. I fumbled around on the table, trying to find the switch, and—

"Alexandria."

I froze in fear and—Wait . . . that voice. "Nebala?"

"Yes." He stepped forward.

I switched on the light, and Nebala used his hand to shield his eyes.

"What are you doing here?" I gasped.

"Scared?" he asked.

I almost said no but realized my reaction had to be etched on my face. How could I not be scared? I'd have liked to see how *he'd* react if I suddenly showed up in *his* hut in the middle of the night. Probably by pulling out a machete or tossing a spear at me. That would be very bad for me. The worst thing that could happen to him was me pummelling him with one of the stuffed animals that lived on my bed.

"How did you get in here?" I asked.

"Window."

"But it's twenty-five feet off the ground. How did you get *up* to the window?" I was wondering if he'd found a ladder in the garage.

"Tree."

"You used the tree? Okay, but how did you get from the tree to my window?"

"Jumped." He pantomimed jumping.

"Nobody could jump that far. That's impossible."

"Possible."

I wanted to argue, but since he was standing right there I had to figure it really was possible.

"Okay, you jumped."

"Yes."

"Are you going to give me anything except one-word answers?"

"Maybe," he said, and then he smiled.

"In that case, let's not worry anymore about *how* you got here. *Why* are you here?"

"Promise."

"Sure, what do you want me to promise?" I asked.

"Not *you* promise. *Me* promise." He pulled out an envelope. "It is from Ruth."

"Ruth sent me a letter!" I exclaimed. "That's wonderful!" I took it from him. "Thanks so much for bringing it all this . . . " Then I had a terrible thought. What was in this letter that was so important it couldn't wait until tomorrow? Had something happened to Ruth . . . or baby Alexandria? I knew that babies in Kenya sometimes did not survive—that was one of the reasons my father had paid to build the clinic.

"Is everybody—Ruth . . . . little Alexandria—is everybody okay?" I asked.

"I do not know."

"What do you mean you don't know?"

"I am here and they are in Africa," he answered. "When I left they were both well . . . but now? I do not know." He shrugged. "I have no gift of far-sight."

From almost anybody else that comment would have seemed strange, sarcastic, or even psychotic. But Nebala was just saying what he meant.

"I'm glad they were fine when you saw them," I said. "But what's so important that you had to bring me the letter tonight?"

"A promise to Ruth and her father that I would give this letter to you at the time of our greetings."

"And you forgot."

He nodded and his eyes fell to the ground. He had forgotten and realized that he had broken his word. To a Maasai that was a terrible, terrible thing because their word was part of their honour, part of who they were. Breaking his word to Ruth was bad, but even worse, he had also given his word to her father—and he was a chief. I knew Nebala would feel awful, even ashamed. It wasn't his fault. With all the travel and everything new and different, he must have been exhausted, confused. It was easy to understand, but excuses like that wouldn't make him feel any better.

"You know," I said, "by bringing the letter to me now you have brought it to me on the day of our greetings, so really, you did keep your promise."

He suddenly looked relieved.

I held out my hand. "Hello, Nebala. I offer you my greetings."

He held out his hand and smiled. "And I offer my greetings to you," he replied. "Thank you. Now I must go."

"Sure. I'll let you out." I didn't want him to set off the alarm system or we'd have my mother up, the security company scrambling, and a call from the police department at the very least. "I'll turn off the alarm for the back door."

"I will go through the window," he said. He walked over.

"No, you don't have to go that way. Let me get the—"

He put a foot up onto the ledge and then jumped out the window!

I sat there, too shocked to move, my mouth hanging open. I struggled to get out of bed, rushing for the window, and I crashed to the floor with a loud thud— my feet were tangled up in the sheets. I kicked them free and crawled and scrambled to the window, pulling myself up and steadying myself as I looked down to the ground. He wasn't there.

I looked over. There he was in the tree, standing on one branch and holding the one above to steady himself.

"See? It's possible," he offered as a brief answer to my unspoken question.

"I can see that." Although I still didn't believe it. "Be careful, you could fall and get hurt."

"I will not fall. I am Maas—"

"Even Maasai can fall, and unless you're a bird you can't fly. Be careful."

He chuckled. "I will be careful. Good night, Alexandria."

"Good night, Nebala."

I watched in awe as he climbed down the tree, disappearing into the branches and foliage until I could make out only little glimpses of him. And then he just disappeared into the darkness. I thought I could hear him—faintly—and maybe I heard him drop to the ground, but I couldn't be sure. I kept looking, waiting for him to set off one of the motion-sensor lights so I could confirm that he was down and safe, but it didn't happen. Apparently Maasai could not only climb a tree like a monkey and leap like a leopard, but also move with such stealth that they didn't even trigger a motion sensor. He was like a ghost. Or a dream. That's what it was like—a dream.

I stood there, thinking that even though I'd seen him, spoken to him, it all still could have passed for a dream because it was nothing short of bizarre. I could just imagine the conversation I'd have with somebody who didn't know about any of this: "Oh yeah, by the way, a Maasai warrior climbed a tree and jumped into my room last night...No, no problem...No, of course I was scared. Wouldn't you be scared? Well, he was just there because he was delivering a letter..." The letter. I'd forgotten!

I grabbed the sheets and duvet and pulled them aside—there it was! I picked it up off the floor and turned it over. On the front, in graceful lettering, it said, "To Alexandria, my sister." That made me smile.

Ruth was Maasai, like Nebala. She lived with her nine brothers and sisters in Kenya, in a village, in a little hut made of mud and cow dung. We'd known each other only a few weeks, and other than a couple of letters we'd had no contact for the past seven months. We had absolutely *nothing* in common—nothing except the fact that we were friends. Good friends.

I opened the envelope and took out the letter, and something fell to the floor. It was a picture. I bent down and picked it up. It was a picture of Ruth holding Alexandria—her baby sister, my namesake. Ruth was smiling and Alexandria was laughing. It looked as though they were sharing a joke.

I stared at the picture. Alexandria was now almost seven months old—which meant she was almost seven months older than when I'd last seen her. I'd been there when she was born, right there. Ruth and her parents believed that if it hadn't been for me, Alexandria wouldn't have lived. Maybe they were right. I'd basically stolen a car to get them to the clinic, and then bullied and threatened and bribed my way to make sure Ruth's mother—baby Alexandria's mother—got the right medical care. Who would have thought that threatening, bribing, bullying, and grand theft auto could have led to something as beautiful as Alexandria?

I unfolded the letter.

Dearest Alexandria,

I hope this letter finds you and your family well. We are all well here, especially your namesake. She is growing so fast, and we all think that she looks more and more like you each day.

I looked at the picture again.

I couldn't really see the resemblance between myself and a seven-month-old black Maasai baby, but I could see how much she *did* look like Ruth. For starters, they shared the same perfect, beautiful eyes. I wished I had those beautiful dark eyes, or at least her nose—straight, with no bump, and with nostrils that were the same size.

I put a hand up to the bump on my nose. Of course that bump wouldn't be there for too, too much longer. My parents had promised me I could have my nose fixed when I turned eighteen, less than two years from now.

Some people might have thought that was vain, but I thought it was exactly the opposite. Anybody who thought they were so perfect that they didn't need to have some surgical adjustments had to be some sort of egomaniac! I could admit that I needed a little help.

I went back to the letter.

The rainy season has failed this year. The land is very brown. Hopefully soon we will have a well and water so we can take care of our crops and our cattle. We know that you and your family will help Nebala and Samuel and Koyati so they can win the money to build our well.

I just hoped we *could* help them. I guessed we could. We were putting them up here in our home, and I'd make sure they could get to the race. That was helping . . . at least as much as I could help, short of running the race for them. Not that that would have been any help at all.

Fresh water will mean so much to everybody. It will be the second miracle that our village has experienced. The first was the building of the clinic. We know how much your family has already done. That is the best news of this letter. The clinic is now finished, and as you can see in the picture, your namesake was the first person seen by the nurse.

I looked back at the picture. I'd been focusing so much on Ruth and Alexandria that I hadn't even noticed where they were. Ruth was sitting on a wooden table—I guess the examination table—and Alexandria was on her lap. In the background was a woman wearing a white lab coat—she had to be the nurse.

Please write back and give the letter to Nebala to deliver. You are in my thoughts and in my prayers.
    Love,
    Ruth

I leaned the picture against the alarm clock on my night table. I really wasn't sure what I could do to help Nebala, but I made a promise to myself then that whatever I could do I *would* do.

CHAPTER NINE

"I just don't understand," Olivia said. "If they want water, why don't they just turn on the tap?"

I swerved the car slightly as I turned to face her.

"Don't you remember anything I told you about my trip to Kenya?" I demanded.

"I remember things."

"Do you remember that the Maasai all live in mud huts?"

"Of course. I'm not an idiot, you know."

Sometimes I wasn't sure about that.

"I just assumed," Olivia said, "that the huts had running water."

"They do have running water."

She gave me a smug look.

"They have running water, if you consider that they have to *run* a mile or so to get it."

I thought back to going with Ruth and the other girls to gather water. We walked for over a mile carrying empty water containers. Then some of the girls went down in a trough dug in the sandy bed of what was a river during the rainy season but was then all dried up. And down there—six feet below the surface—was a little puddle of muddy water. The containers were filled and hauled back up and then carried back to the huts, where that dirty water was used for cleaning and cooking and drinking. A shudder went up my spine thinking about it.

"That's why they're all such good runners," I explained. "They walk or run everywhere. The Maasai say they can walk without stopping from sunrise to sunset."

"Really?" Olivia asked.

"Don't ever doubt it when a Maasai says he's going to do something."

"So you believe they can win the marathon?" she asked.

"Of course they can," I replied. Actually, up until that moment I hadn't even thought about it. "What I can't believe is that they sold their cattle to get here."

"We sold my horse," she said.

"It isn't the same thing!" I snapped. "Cattle are very important to them."

"Blackie was very important to me."

"You don't understand."

"Apparently I don't understand *anything*," she said.

We drove along in silence, and I could sense her starting to pout in the seat next to me. Part of me wanted to just enjoy the silence, but she was my friend.

"I'm sorry," I said. "I'm just a little bit thrown by them suddenly appearing. It's my fault for not explaining things well enough. Would it be all right if I explained about the Maasai and cattle?"

"If you think I'm smart enough to understand."

"Don't be like that, *Oli*," I said, using her little-kid nickname. "You're one of the smartest people I know." A small lie.

She straightened up in her seat. "Please, I'd love to hear."

"The Maasai don't collect cars, or homes, or money. They collect cows. The man who has the most cows is the richest man in the village."

"So cows are a status symbol, a way of keeping track of who's winning," she said. "And when they sold all their cows they became the poorest men in the village, right?"

"It's even more than that. When they sold their cows it's almost like they stopped being men and became boys again."

"Really?"

"Really."

"So when they sold all their cows to come here it was like they were giving up being men," she said.

"I knew you'd understand. I'm sure when they win the race they'll use the money to put in the well but also to buy back their cattle," I explained.

"That makes sense," she said. "But what if they *don't* win?"

"Then I guess they can't put in the well."

"Or buy back their cows," she said.

Suddenly I was hit in the head by what she'd said. If they couldn't buy back their cattle, they couldn't become men again. There was no choice. They had to win the race. They *had* to. They were Maasai. They could do anything. Couldn't they?

"My street," Olivia said.

"What?"

"You just drove past my street!"

"Sorry," I said as I slowed the car down. "I guess I just wasn't thinking."

"Or you were thinking about something else."

I turned the car around and headed down her street.

"I promised Nebala that I'd take them to register for the marathon tomorrow. Do you want to come with us?" I asked.

"Of course. I wouldn't miss that for money."

"Yes, you would, if it was enough money," I said.

She shrugged. "Or the perfect pair of jeans . . . But I do want to come. What time are you heading down?"

"Around eleven."

"Could you pick me up on the way?"

"Sure. How long before you get your car back?"

"My mother said something about when hell freezes over, but my father is starting to soften. I still can't believe they took my car away to begin with."

"I still can't believe you thought they wouldn't after your second accident and fifth speeding ticket."

I drove through the front gate of her house and up the driveway.

"They weren't serious accidents. It wasn't like anybody was injured."

I stopped directly in front of the door. Olivia reached over and we hugged and exchanged air kisses and then she climbed out of the car.

"The race is this weekend, right?" she asked.

"Yes, on Sunday."

"So what are you going to do with them until then?"

"I haven't really thought about that," I admitted.

"Are you going to school tomorrow? I mean, after we do the registration thing?" Olivia asked.

"I should go to school, but I really can't leave them alone at home."

"Then the solution is simple," she said. "Bring them!"

"I can't do that."

"Why not?" she asked.

"Just . . . not a great idea."

"You're probably right." She ran up to her front door, then turned and called out, with a laugh, "Still, wouldn't they be the coolest show-and-tell of all time?"

Cracked me up just thinking about it!

CHAPTER TEN

I adjusted the rear-view mirror so I could see all three of my Maasai in the back seat. Nebala sat there quietly with a serious and thoughtful look on his face. Koyati also looked as though he was thinking—thinking about hurting somebody. That was his usual expression, though, so it probably didn't mean a thing. Maybe he was just practising getting his game face on for the race. And then there was Samuel—big grin, eyes wide open, looking all around, his head turning from side to side. He was the yin to Koyati's yang. He never stopped smiling.

I turned onto Olivia's street and almost instantly saw her standing by the curb in front of her house. That was not a good sign. It usually meant that her parents were going at it again. They were having a nasty time. She'd told me that they were *working on their marriage.* That was the line my parents had always used, just before they'd stopped working on the marriage and started working on the divorce. At least they'd found something they were both good at.

I pulled up right beside her.

"*Jambo!*" she called out as she climbed in.

"How is it shaking, *dude*?" Samuel said.

"If you think I'm a *dude*, I'm definitely doing something wrong," Olivia replied with a cute grin.

Nebala chuckled at that, which was all the encouragement Olivia needed.

"Seriously, though," she said, "are you sure this guy isn't from Malibu instead of Kenya?"

"No surf where he comes from," I replied.

I shifted the car into drive and we started off.

"Are you really okay to come with us today?" I asked Olivia quietly.

"Yeah, it's a good time to get out of the house," she replied.

"How bad?"

"No worse than usual. I just wish they'd stop pretending and get it over with," she said.

"It could work out."

She laughed. "Yeah, like that's gonna happen."

"Some marriages do work."

"Really? How many friends do we have whose parents are married?" she asked.

"Lots."

"I mean married to each other, first-time marriage, husband and wife who are the mother and father of the children who live with them."

"Well . . . there's your parents."

She laughed even louder, but it wasn't a happy laugh. "On the bright side, I see a lot of guilt presents in my future."

I glanced at her. She was shaking a little and I could see that tears were starting to form in her eyes. I also noticed that she wasn't wearing her seatbelt.

"Belt up," I said. "I wouldn't want anything to happen to you."

She reached over and snapped on her belt. "It's nice to know that somebody cares about me."

"Your parents care about you."

"It certainly doesn't show."

"They still care. Just . . . hang in there," I offered.

"Maybe you should also be talking to somebody else about his seatbelt," she said, motioning to the back seat.

I looked in my rear-view mirror. Once again Samuel was standing up, his arms outstretched like wings.

"Make him sit down!" I yelled.

Nebala reached out and pulled him down.

"And he should put his seatbelt on . . . All of you should be belted in so you don't get hurt or killed!"

"We are not afraid of being killed," Nebala said.

"Yeah, yeah, yeah, I know. You're Maasai and you're not afraid of anything. Put on your seatbelts anyway."

There was grumbling in Swahili, words I couldn't understand, but I understood the attitude. I suddenly felt like the mother of three badly behaved children. If they were going to act that role then I'd act mine.

I slammed on the brakes and pulled over to the side

of the road. The three of them tumbled forward, smashing into the back of the seats and practically tumbling over into the front.

Slowly I turned around. "I am not going anywhere until you put on your seatbelts."

Nebala glared at me—a glare to match Koyati's. Samuel rubbed his head where it had struck the back of the seat, but he was still smiling.

"I'm not playing. Put on your seatbelts . . . *now.*"

Nebala's stare and glare intensified, and I suddenly realized that telling a Maasai warrior—*three* Maasai warriors—what to do was probably not my brightest move. They didn't really take orders very well from anybody, and especially not from a woman . . . well, a girl. Maybe I should just let them not wear them. What harm was it going to do?

Suddenly Nebala reached over. I jumped, and a little shriek escaped my lips. He looked confused, then amused. He took the end of one of the seatbelts and pulled it over Samuel, clicking it, locking him in place.

"He will stay in his seat."

"Thanks."

"Now you can drive," he said. "Make it so, Number One."

Oh, very funny. I'd almost forgotten about his thing for *Star Trek.*

"Yes, Captain Picard. Now I'll drive."

I started to pull away from the curb and a car blared its horn. I slammed on the brakes as it swerved past me. I hadn't seen it at all. The driver of the convertible lifted his hand high into the air as he drove off, one finger raised even higher.

"What a jerk!" Olivia exclaimed.

"I should have looked," I said. "I was distracted."

I adjusted my rear-view mirror once again so I could see behind the car instead of into the back seat.

"Keep an eye on them," I whispered to Olivia, and she nodded.

Olivia sat sideways in her seat so she could watch our Maasai passengers. I looked in the rear-view and the side-view, shoulder-checked, and then eased into traffic when there was a gap.

"I really appreciate your coming along today," I told Olivia.

"I wouldn't want to miss this."

"Well, it's not going to be that interesting. We're just bringing the guys down to register for the race."

She laughed. "Something tells me that walking in with these three is going to be pretty interesting, no matter what."

"I guess you're right. Still, you know . . . thanks."

"Hey, that's what friends do."

Olivia *was* my friend. A *real* friend. Not just somebody who was in my class or went to my school or who I shopped with or went to the same parties with—although she was all of those. She was more.

Before I went to Africa I would have told you that I had dozens and dozens of friends. And Olivia certainly wouldn't have ranked very high on that food chain. But when I came back I saw things through new eyes. All that stupid shopping, the desperate need for just the right thing to wear, the cars, the parties, the pettiness, the gossip—everybody talking but nobody actually saying anything—the fascination over such meaningless nonsense, the . . . the . . . everything.

I think—no, I *know*—that I felt disgusted by it all. After seeing people who survived on so little—and seemed so happy despite it all—I had no time for people who had everything but didn't seem to be happy.

For the first month I was back I didn't even shop. I didn't set foot in a mall or even go down to Rodeo Drive, once known to me as the happiest place in the world, forget Disneyland. I hardly wore any makeup, stopped watching reality TV and reading the celebrity mags. I went to parties, but I didn't really enjoy myself. I had absolutely *nothing* in common with the people I was hanging out with. And I told them.

I told them about the poverty and problems in Africa. I told them about what they could do about it. I told them about the things they were doing that were wrong, or shallow, or silly—and that was pretty well everything. But nobody wanted to hear about starving children when they were eating their sushi. Nobody wanted to be told about people who didn't have fresh drinking water while they were sipping on a double-shot latte with cinnamon sprinkles. Nobody wanted to be told about people who didn't have shoes when they were so delighted that they'd finally got their hands on the new Birkin bag. I knew all that because I was the one telling them those things. Time and time again.

Looking back with the insight of a few passing months, I realized that the post-Africa version of me was, without a doubt, the most annoying, pretentious, obnoxious person imaginable. And believe me, I could have been accused of those same faults before I went away, only in a different way.

In those first four weeks I lost a lot of friends. Well, really, I didn't lose *any* friends. What I lost were a lot of people who I'd thought were my friends but really only occupied the same physical space as me. And through it all, no matter what a pain I was, regardless of how preachy I became, Olivia was still there standing by me.

So she was right; I did care about her. She was a good person—sometimes a good person hidden beneath a layer of designer clothes, expensive makeup, and a shield of the most pretentious accessories money could buy—but still, a good person, and my best friend.

And I think through her I sort of found my balance. I would never forget what I had seen and experienced—the people I'd met in Africa and the way they lived their lives—but there was no point in telling everybody about it . . . well, *lecturing* them about it, all the time.

Even worse, I couldn't tell anyone about my family's donation to build the medical clinic near Ruth's village. It was important for her village, and really, what was that kind of money to my father? For *most* of the people who lived in my neighbourhood, it might have been the cost of their *fifth* car, or the gardening service, or their monthly clothing allowance, or the personal chef. But I'd quickly discovered that telling people what we'd done only made them feel uncomfortable. Maybe they realized that it was something they could do quite easily if they really wanted to. It wasn't the means they were lacking but the will to help. Why couldn't these people see or understand how even a little would mean so much to people who— No, I couldn't let myself get wound up. No point.

I pulled into the parking lot and searched for a spot. I knew I was in the right place because the people around us walked like runners, looked like runners, and worst of all, *dressed* like runners—and by that I mean *horribly*. Sure, I'd come to understand that fashion isn't *everything*, but surely it had to be *something*.

When we climbed out of the car, I was suddenly, along with Olivia, a little island of style adrift in a sea of fashion disasters. What was it about runners that made them want—no, *need*—to dress so totally repulsively? I understood that when they were running they couldn't very well dress in Gucci and Miu Miu shoes. But today they weren't running; they were simply registering to run. Did they think the organizers wouldn't let them participate unless they dressed the part? Did they think that if they looked halfway fashionable they would be sent home?

People passed by dressed in skimpy little shorts, mesh shirts—I couldn't even *think* of an occasion when mesh might be considered clothing—and lots of tight spandex bodysuits. Goodness, put on little whiskers and ears and they would have looked like they were wearing cat costumes—and I'm not talking a sort of Halle Berry Catwoman. More like a cat costume that would have been turned down by a six-year-old at Hallowe'en. And the colours! Did running make you colour-blind? Really, who decided that lime green and orange were a good combination? Come to think of it, if I dressed like that I'd run too—run away where nobody could see me!

Not that I would ever be a runner. It's a completely impractical mode of transportation. If you want to enjoy the view, you walk. If you want to get some- where, you drive. If you want to catch the eye of the opposite sex, you work on your strut. I know runners who talk about the peace and tranquility of running, but I just tell them about the peace and tranquility of a full body wrap and shiatsu massage. For me, running has to have some purpose—a sale at the mall, perhaps, and rushing in when the doors first open. Of course, having been in Africa, I can now say from first-hand experience that being chased by a four-thousand- pound elephant is sufficient motivation to make anyone run like an Olympic sprinter.

Then there was their choice of footwear—totally clunky and totally unattractive, and apparently made with all sorts of space-age materials and adorned with garish little swooshy symbols and stripes. Couldn't they replace the swooshy symbol with some sort of animal? Perhaps a cheetah? No, cheetahs are fast but have no endurance, and the marathon is all about endurance—twenty-six miles of it.

I looked at Nebala and it came to me—running shoes should have a little Maasai on the side!

Not that Nebala and Samuel and Koyati were wearing running shoes. They wore simple sandals that were actually crafted from pieces of recycled tires. Yes, they wore tire tread for footwear. I wasn't sure if that was completely inappropriate or completely and utterly correct. Of course I didn't think anybody was noticing their tire-tread shoes because the brilliant red blankets and dress pretty well captured everybody's attention.

My plan had been to simply fall in with the flow of people to find our way, but as usual, everyone was just standing and staring at the guys in their Maasai wardrobe.

"Excuse me," I asked a man, obviously a runner. "Can you tell me where we can find the registration desk?"

"For the marathon?" he asked.

"No, for the fashion show!" Olivia snapped.

"Yes, the marathon," I said before his confused look took hold.

"For all of you?" he asked.

"Just three of us."

I noticed that the crowd of fashion rejects around us was growing quickly. Then I looked at Nebala. I knew that attached to his belt, hidden underneath his blanket, he had his *konga* with him. In a fight between three Maasai warriors and three hundred runners, I'd bet on the Maasai.

Then again, it wasn't going to be that sort of fight. It was going to be three Maasai running against three thousand other runners ... No, not three thousand— there might be ten times that many. I'd seen marathons on TV, and they were just masses of people. I remembered something about there being forty thousand people in the New York City Marathon. *Forty thousand.* There couldn't be that many running in Beverly Hills. . . . It wasn't a big city like New York or . . . well, really, it *was* L.A. The richest part of L.A. Could there be that many people who were going to be part of this run? Serious runners, people who, with their crew of personal coaches, trained for years and years? People from around the world? Could Nebala and his friends outrun people like that who devoted their lives to running?

I got a sick feeling in the pit of my stomach. Nebala and his friends had come here to win—*certain* that they could win. But what if they couldn't? I didn't want to think about that. After all, they did spend their entire lives walking and running. They trained not just hours every day, but *every* hour, *every* day. Nebala had told me about how Samuel had once tracked a wounded lion for three days, covering hundreds of miles, before he finally killed it. Anybody who could do that could do this, no problem.

"Just come with me," the man said. "I'm on my way to register right now."

"Thank you."

We fell in behind him. The crowd opened up at one end and allowed us through. Then everybody fell in behind us. I felt like a celebrity followed by a horde of paparazzi. It did have that quality. Everybody was watching us, and there were a lot of phones being pulled out and pictures taken. Of course I was only in the shots because I was standing beside the celebrities. I guess that made me part of the posse. No, not the posse—more like the Maasai's entourage!

CHAPTER ELEVEN

As we walked, the crowd moved aside for us, snapped pictures, and then followed along behind. It was a combination of Moses parting the Red Sea, a celebrity reality show, and the Pied Piper leading the rat parade—except a whole bunch of these runners seemed to weigh *less* than a rat. Forget supermodels being too thin, these runners all looked downright scrawny. I guess the difference between them and the models was that these people were all incredibly fit—they just looked like they really needed a couple of good meals.

Up ahead there were big signs that said "REGISTRATION"—no more question where we were headed.

"Are these guys, like, real Maasai?" our escort asked.

"As opposed to fake Maasai?" I questioned.

"I mean, like, they're really from Africa?"

"From Africa, from Kenya."

"Kenyans! They are the best marathon runners in the world," he said, clearly in awe.

"Cheruiyot!" said Nebala proudly.

"Tanui!" cheered Samuel. "Cherigat!"

Our runner friend seemed to recognize what they were saying—runners' names, I guessed?

"Yeah," he said. "Kenyan runners won the Boston Marathon ten years in a row! Maybe I shouldn't bother even entering," he added.

"No harm in entering," Olivia said. "Unless you were hoping to win, of course."

He looked both disappointed and amused by her remark. I just hoped she was right.

We entered the building. There were tables arranged around the room, and above each were letters of the alphabet.

"Have your friends pre-registered?" our guide asked.

I looked at Nebala. He looked as though he didn't understand the question.

"Have you already filled out papers?" I asked.

"We have papers."

"Oh, good. Can I have them?"

He reached inside his garment and pulled out a sheaf of papers. He started sorting through them. Some of them were worn and torn and tattered. He could have really used something like a cool leather messenger bag in a colour that would be complementary to the red of his clothes . . . maybe a tan, or— What was I talking about? As if he was going to carry something like an oversized man-purse. A spear, a shield, a bow and arrow—yes. A trendy bag—no.

He finally found a page and handed it to me. It was the information sheet about the marathon, the one he'd already shown me back at the house.

"No, not this," I explained. "Did you send in any registration papers before you came? If you did, we can probably skip at least some of this craziness."

He shook his head. "Is this a problem?"

"No—that's what we're here for." I eyed the crowds up ahead. Maybe we wouldn't have to wait after all. "Just come with me."

I took Nebala by the hand and dragged him toward the registration desk. Samuel and Koyati fell in behind . . . followed by our giant fan club.

"Excuse me!" I called out, and again the crowds parted, all the way to the desk. "These three need to register for the marathon."

The man behind the desk had his head down; he was filling out some papers. "Just hold on until I finish with—" He looked up and his mouth dropped open.

"We need to register these three for the marathon," I said.

"Register?"

"Yes, this *is* the registration desk, isn't it?"

"Um . . . well, uh, yes," he sputtered.

"And that is what you do, isn't it? That's why you're sitting here, correct?"

"Yes, of course."

He scrambled for some papers and handed me one set, then a second and a third. "Have them fill out these forms . . . over there." He gestured to some tables where other people were sitting down with their paperwork.

I took the papers, and Olivia and the guys followed me over to the tables. I looked for a pen . . . none. I almost asked Nebala if he had one, but I didn't want to risk embarrassing him. A *konga* he had—a pen, probably not.

"Does anybody have a pen we can use?" I called out.

Suddenly half a dozen pens were thrust into my face. Helpful . . . but where did runners carry pens? Oh, yeah, in their fanny packs.

I handed a pen to each of the guys. "You need to fill out these forms to register for the race," I said.

They all nodded their heads in agreement and smiled, but nobody started to write. Wait . . . could they write? Nebala had gone to college, so of course he could write, but I didn't know about the other two. What I did know was that nobody was filling out the forms. Nebala wasn't writing, but he was reading, studying the form as if it were some kind of test. Koyati wasn't even looking at the form, and he was holding the pen as if it were a knife. Was he planning on stabbing the questions he didn't like?

I was trying to figure out how to ask about their literacy skills with the least possible cringe factor, but Olivia decided to just go for it.

"You three do know how to write, don't you?" she asked.

"Samuel and Koyati read and write in two languages," Nebala said.

"That's great!" I said. "So they can—"

"The languages are Swahili and Maa," Nebala explained. "I can read and write in *three* languages. I also read and write in English."

"That's great. So I can help Samuel, and Olivia can help Koyati."

Olivia gave me a dirty look. That wasn't nice, but Samuel was, and Koyati still sort of scared me a little.

"I can write," Nebala said, "but I do not understand what all these things mean."

"Forms can be difficult," I agreed. "Which part is confusing?"

He put his finger against the form—what looked like the very first line. "What does this mean?"

I turned my head so I could see where he was pointing. "Name," I read out loud. "You don't know what to put down for your name?" That wasn't the part I'd expected to confuse anybody.

"What does this mean?" he asked.

"Surname. That means your last name."

"I am Nebala."

"Yes, and I'm Alexandria . . . Alexandria *Hyatt*. Hyatt is my *surname*." He didn't reply. I wondered. "Do you have a last name?"

"I am *Nebala*."

"But there must be more than one Nebala at home. How do they know it's you and not another Nebala?"

"I am Nebala, oldest son of *King* Nebala."

I looked at the form. There were a dozen or so little spaces. Certainly not enough to put down all of that. Wait! I filled in "Nebala" for first name and then simply put in one word for his surname: "King."

I ran my finger down the form. If surname was a problem, I couldn't imagine how much more difficult the rest of it was going to be. All the usual stuff—address, zip code, and phone number—were not going to be that usual. I had a feeling that it was going to take me almost as long to complete these forms as it was going to take them to actually run the marathon.

We worked away at if for a while, and when Olivia and I had finally filled in all the blanks we could, we handed the forms back. There were a few missing sections, but we'd done our best.

"Fine," said the man behind the desk "Three entries. That will be six hundred dollars."

"Six hundred dollars!" I exclaimed.

"Two hundred per entry."

I turned to Nebala. He pulled out a little bag that was hanging from his neck. It wasn't Coach or Chanel, but it did look like a purse . . . sort of like the little change purse my grandmother used to carry in her handbag. He opened the drawstring and started to remove a stack of bills. But they didn't look right. They looked more like Monopoly money. No, they were Kenyan shillings.

I did a quick calculation—I was very good at mental math. The current exchange rate was 61 Kenyan shillings to one U.S. dollar. So $600 worked out to 36,600 shillings. I watched as Nebala counted out the bills and placed them on the table—40,000 shillings. That emptied out his little purse. When he got his change he'd have only 3,400 shillings left, or $55.73. Not very much. I guessed he had other money somewhere else. I hoped.

"What are these?" the man behind the table asked.

"Money," Nebala said.

The man picked up one of the bills and looked at it quizzically, then laughed. "This isn't *real* money."

Nebala scowled. "This is good money." He pushed the stack toward the man.

"I mean we don't take foreign money. Only U.S. currency or credit cards. Do you have any credit cards?"

I almost laughed.

"Here, put it on this," Olivia said. She snapped down a gold American Express card.

"Do you have enough room on your card for this?" I asked.

"I have all the room I want. Divorcing-parent guilt goes a long way."

The man reached for the card, but before he could take it Nebala put his hand down, pinning the card and the man's hand. He tried to remove his hand, but Nebala held it firmly in place.

"What are you doing?" the man squeaked.

"Take the money . . . Our money is *good*." Both Samuel and Koyati moved closer.

The man now looked confused. What he should have looked was scared. He had insulted a Maasai warrior—no, *three* warriors. He didn't know how quickly this could turn ugly.

He struggled to move his hand again, but Nebala reached over with his other hand and grabbed him by

the wrist, stopping him. The man now had the good
sense to look scared.

"But you *are* paying," I said to Nebala.

I squeezed myself between Nebala and the table,
then took his hand and tried to lift it up. I couldn't
budge it. He had the man's hand trapped beneath his.

"Olivia wants the money. She wishes to have some
Kenyan money because someday she wants to go with
me to Kenya . . . right, Olivia?"

"I would *love* to go to Kenya."

"See? She wants the Kenyan shillings, and she'll put
the six hundred dollars on her card. You're still paying."

I could see Nebala relax, and I was able to lift up
his hand at last.

The man removed his hand and rubbed his wrist
with the other.

"Please put it on her card," I said.

Tentatively he reached over and took the card. He
looked relieved when Nebala didn't try to stop him.
He ran it through the machine, took out the little
strip of paper, and handed it to Olivia. She signed it
and handed it back. He took one copy, handed it to
her, and placed the second with the three forms, stap-
ling it to the top of one.

"So is this it?" I asked. "Are they registered?"

"Yes, just take these three receipts over to the next
table and they'll receive their race packages."

"Thank you," I replied. "You've been very helpful."

We turned and started to walk away. I wasn't sure
who was more grateful we were leaving, him or me.

"Wait!" the man called out.

I turned around. What could he possibly want? Obviously Nebala hadn't scared him enough.

He was holding up his copy of one of the forms, and he came around the table toward us. "You failed to complete the *qualifying* section."

"There were a few sections that didn't make sense to us."

"But this section is *essential*. We have to know what other races they have competed in."

"They haven't run any other races," I said.

"What?" he demanded. "No other races?"

"None. That's why it's blank. This will be their first."

"But to be able to run in this marathon they have to have been in other marathons and made the qualifying time."

"Qualifying time? What are you talking about?"

"There are standards," he snapped. "To qualify to run in the Beverly Hills Marathon you have to have previously run at least a 3:05."

"A what?"

He shook his head and gave me a look that could only be described as disgusted. "You have to have run another marathon and finished in less than three hours and five minutes."

"Is that even possible?" I asked.

"That is a high standard—five minutes less than to qualify for the Boston Marathon—but very, very doable."

"I'm sure they've run that fast before," I said. "They are Maasai."

"I don't care what they are," he said. "They need documentation."

"But they don't have any documentation!" I protested.

"Then I'll need those back." He reached out and tried to grab the registration forms from me. I held on tightly, and he struggled to rip them out of my hands. He bent my hand back and he pushed.

"Stop . . . you're hurting—"

Koyati leaped forward with lightning speed, and before I could say a word, he pushed the man backwards. Instantly he released my hand. Koyati pushed him back until he was pinned against the wall, standing on his tippy-toes, his feet almost off the ground. Our Maasai warrior was holding him in place with one hand pressed against his throat. The man's eyes were bugged out, and now, finally, he looked as scared as he should have been.

Olivia let out a scream, and the people who hadn't seen what *had* happened were now all watching what *was* happening . . . and wondering if something worse was *about* to happen.

"Koyati," I called out, and he looked at me. "Could you let him down . . . please?" I asked sweetly.

He didn't respond. He continued to glare at the man. It was then I noticed that his free hand was hidden beneath his blanket. That could mean only one thing—it was holding on to a weapon. This could quickly go from bad to deadly.

I put my hand on Koyati's arm, the one pinning the man—who was now starting to turn a little blue. Hopefully all that running had given him extra lung capacity.

"I'm okay . . . Please let him down."

Nebala barked out a few words in Swahili. Koyati let out a big sigh, like he was disappointed, and then released him.

The man slumped against the wall. He rubbed his throat and then took in a very, very loud and deep breath.

"Are you all right?" I asked.

"He . . . he . . . choked me!"

"He was just protecting me," I said. "But let's not fight about that. We need to talk . . . well, not me and you. I need to speak to whoever is in charge. Right now."

He nodded in agreement. That was smart. At least he was finally scared.

CHAPTER TWELVE

I settled into the seat. Soft leather. Imported. Expensive. Probably Italian. I looked around the room. The furniture was simple but elegant, expensive, well chosen. One wall was lined with books—probably just for show, more leather. The walls were decorated with artwork, tasteful, understated, the colours working beautifully with both the furniture and the walls. Whoever this office belonged to had taste. And money.

The door opened and a man walked in. He was in his middle to late twenties. Perfect hair, perfect complexion, perfectly put together designer clothes, matching and coordinated down to his leather Gucci loafers—I recognized them as this year's most up-to-date style and worth serious coin. I didn't know who he was, but he certainly wasn't one of the runners—not with those clothes and those shoes and that sense of style.

He walked with a sense of confidence. Not a strut, but understated. His walk said, "I'm well respected, well connected, and . . . well, just plain rich." I knew that walk. I *had* that walk. Olivia and I exchanged a knowing look—we were getting a good idea now of who we were up against, and we'd met his type before.

He did a comical sort of double-take when he saw the Maasai standing behind my chair, but he covered it well. Then he flashed a smile—perfect teeth with white veneers. Probably twenty thousand dollars' worth of dental. He extended his hand to me.

"Good afternoon," he sang out. "My name is Dakota . . . Dakota Rivers. And you are?"

"Alexandria Hyatt," I said as we shook.

"Hyatt?" he questioned. "You wouldn't, by any chance, be related to the Hyatts of Newport?"

"My father has cousins. Evan and Eleanor."

"Yes, of course. They have a place on the water."

"I think I remember my father telling me something about them having a little beach house."

"Little? It is *quite* the home."

"I guess we all have different definitions of little," I said, trying to let him know that I was a few rungs up the social ladder from his friends, our cousins.

"Have you never been there?" he asked.

I shook my head.

"I've been to a number of summer soirees at their home. Wonderful hosts. I'll pass on my regards the next time I see them."

"Thank you."

"It is such a small world," he said.

"Yes. Definitely."

I inhaled. He even smelled expensive. I thought that I recognized the scent. "You wouldn't, by chance, be wearing Lalique Pour Homme 'Le Faune,' would you?"

He flashed me another perfect smile. "That is truly impressive. Obviously you are a woman not only of discerning taste, but of fine olfactory talents."

"It's one of my favourites," I said. "Now my turn."

He leaned forward until he was almost touching me. He was so close that I could feel the warmth of his body. He inhaled.

"Yes, that does smell familiar . . . very feminine . . . a certain elegance."

I felt myself get a little flushed.

"I believe it's Dolce and Gabbana."

"Yes, it is!"

"Our turn to be impressed," Olivia said.

He turned to Olivia now, all charm. "My apologies for not introducing myself to you as well!" Dakota said.

"This is my friend Olivia."

They shook hands.

"Enchanted to meet you."

"And these three are Nebala, Samuel, and Koyati."

He offered his hand. Nobody reached to take it. They just stood there, stock-still, silent, and scowling scarily.

"It's a pleasure to meet you," he said, withdrawing his hand and bowing his head slightly. Not bad. He'd managed to rescue himself from an embarrassment. I could work with this man. If he'd been a few years younger or I'd been a few years older we could perhaps have done more than just work. He was hot.

"Please, let's all just take a seat and discuss this unfortunate *situation*."

He sat down behind his desk, and the three Maasai continued to stand behind us.

"My assistant, Jarrett, gave me some information about what happened," Dakota said. "That was quite the scene out there."

"It was," I agreed.

"Jarrett is very upset."

"I think we're all upset."

"First off, I want to let you know that I have discussed things with him, and while he has been urging me to get the police involved, I am certain that I can convince him to simply ignore the whole incident."

"Really?" I said.

"Certainly. This is very much a courtesy to you, Alexandria, and the relationship I have with your Newport cousins. We'll simply forget that any of this happened, and you and your friends are free to leave."

"That's so generous," I offered, and he smiled, "but I'm afraid I can't simply forget what happened. I'm afraid I will have to press charges against Jarrett for assaulting me."

"What?" Dakota gasped. For a split second he looked confused and panicked, but then that look of cool returned. "I'm sorry. I am not sure what you mean."

"He grabbed me by the arm, trying to take away these forms." I held them up. "Thank goodness that Koyati was present and stopped him from assaulting me further."

"That certainly isn't the way that Jarrett reported

the incident," Dakota said. "And other employees have corroborated his story."

"And I have witnesses who can corroborate mine. Isn't that right, Olivia?"

"I'm not exactly sure what 'corroborate' means, but whatever Alexandria says is the truth."

"Perhaps we *should* let the police settle this," Dakota said. He smiled again, but it wasn't the charming smile. It was more smug.

"Perhaps we *should*." I pulled out my phone. "Do you have the number of the Beverly Hills Police Department?" I asked.

"Umm . . . no, I don't." His smug little smile was gone.

"And while I'm at it, I should also call the newspaper and tell them about the assault on a young girl by an employee of the—"

"Perhaps we should all take a moment to pause," he said. "It might be in the best interests of all parties if we simply dealt with this in this room."

"That would be better," I said. "So we're in agreement that nobody is going to contact the police . . . correct?"

"Correct," he agreed.

I tried not to smile because I knew it would be my turn to look smug and self-satisfied. This guy had tried to bluff me into backing down, and he was the one who'd just turned and run with his tail between his legs.

"You have to appreciate that this is the first year of the event," Dakota said. "As with all new events, there is a certain learning curve, and mistakes will be made."

"And I'm sure that under your leadership, they will also be corrected."

"Very kind of you," he said.

Now that I'd threatened him with a stick it was time to use a carrot. There was hardly a male alive who couldn't be manipulated through food, flattery, or flirtation.

"It is so unfortunate," I said, "that we are meeting under these conditions rather than while sipping a cool drink on the veranda of my cousins' beach house."

"That would be a better first meeting."

"Sadly, we can't change the circumstances of our first meeting, but perhaps we can, at some time in the future, arrange for a more pleasant second meeting."

He flashed me that beautiful smile and his cheeks dimpled, and I could have sworn that there was a little twinkle in his eyes.

"We can only hope. Regardless, I am pleased to be dealing with one of these minor problems with an individual such as you," he said sweetly.

"Thank you."

"Someone with such obvious style and taste. If I have to have a disagreement—even such a minor one—it is a pleasure to have that disagreement with a person such as you."

"Again, thank you."

"This is a very important year for the marathon, being its inaugural year. A good first impression is so important."

"My mother always says that," I said.

"A wise woman." He paused. "We are competing against the established races. When you think of marathons, what cities come to mind?"

I really couldn't think of any.

"New York and Boston," Olivia chimed in.

"Exactly!" Dakota exclaimed.

Points for Olivia. She was always surprising me.

"They have history and tradition, and more important, brand recognition. I'm sure you can appreciate the value of brand recognition," he said to me.

I nodded my head. To a lot of people, the quality of the name on the label was often more important than the quality of the product itself—although I tried to think a little differently these days.

"But we have higher standards. Someone such as you would realize just exactly what we're trying to do here. We really are trying to be a cut above."

He gestured to the banner that occupied the wall to my right. It read: "*Beverly Hills Marathon . . . A Cut Above the Rest.*"

"That is more than just a motto. That is our goal. We want the Beverly Hills Marathon to represent what this community is about. Style, taste, class, elegance—qualities I know you can truly appreciate."

"Well . . ." I said. There was no point in arguing with that.

"And that is why we set our standards so high. Higher than anybody else's. Our qualifying time is faster than either the Boston or the New York marathon. You have to be more qualified and a better runner to compete in Beverly Hills than in either of

those two races." He paused. "I'm sure you can understand our need to have such high standards."

"Of course."

"I'm so glad. So you understand why your friends
cannot compete."

"That makes perfect— What?" I exclaimed.

"Why your friends cannot compete. They not only
haven't met the qualifying time, but in fact have no
race results at all. This is not a beginner's race. This is
the Beverly Hills Marathon . . . *a cut above.*"

He had taken me so much by surprise that I
didn't even know what to say. Who had been playing
who, here?

"But as an act of good faith, we will provide special
passes for all of you! You can go to the party tonight,
have full access to the VIP tent during the race, be part
of the after-party, and partake, free of charge, of course,
of all food and refreshments. There will be lobster
flown in from the East Coast, caviar, champagne—"

"Excuse me," I said, cutting him off.

I flipped open my phone again and pushed 2
on the speed-dial. It rang once, then twice, and then
I pushed the button to put it on speakerphone.

"Hello," came a voice after the third ring.

"Daddy."

"Hello, angel."

"Daddy, I have a problem," I said in my best little-
girl voice.

"We can't have that. Tell me what I can do to take
care of that problem."

"I need you to come down here right now."

"Down where?"

I turned to Dakota. "Where exactly are we?"

"Um . . . 158 Wilshire Boulevard."

"Did you get that, Daddy?"

"Yes. But, Alexandria, are you in trouble?"

"Not me, but my friends. They need your help."

"What sort of help?" he asked.

"They need you to *sue* somebody. Please come quickly."

Before he could say anything I hung up the phone.

I looked over at Dakota. "This is going to be messy . . . *very* messy."

CHAPTER THIRTEEN

"Okay, is that everything?" my father asked.

"Everything."

It had taken just over an hour for my father to get down to Wilshire Boulevard, and then less than ten minutes for me to explain things to him, sitting in the lounge area outside Dakota's office. That was pretty fast talking, since I'd also had to explain why I was sitting in a fancy Beverly Hills office building with three fierce-looking Maasai warriors.

Periodically, while we were talking, Dakota stuck his head out of his office and glared at us. I didn't look directly back, but I could see him out of the corner of my eye. He had become progressively less happy and more angry-looking. I was glad that the Maasai were the only ones with weapons.

"You're sure there's nothing else?" my father

asked again. "I need to have all the information."

"I've told you everything."

He gave me a look, as though he was still question-ing me.

"I don't do that anymore," I said. "I don't lie, and I don't leave anything out."

I used to do both to get my way. But this time I'd told him everything.

"I wasn't really doubting you," he said.

"Yes, you were, but that's okay . . . You have good reason not to trust me."

"I *had* good reason. Not anymore."

Things *had* changed, partly thanks to our once-a-week therapy nights. No matter what my parents were doing—even my super-busy businessman father—they came and they talked. Funny, my parents got along better now than they ever had when they were "happily married." I couldn't help thinking that if we'd started therapy years ago maybe they never would have got divorced. No point in thinking about that, though. "Happily divorced" seemed to agree with both of them.

"Then let's meet with this man. And, Alexandria, let me do the talking."

I pulled a pretend zipper across my lips.

He got up, and the five of us also rose to our feet.

"You know," my father said, "it might be better if not *all* of us took part in this meeting."

Instantly I understood what my father meant. Having Nebala in there might be okay, but I could just see Koyati pulling out his *konga* and taking a swing at the guy.

"Perhaps it would be best if it was just me," he said.

"No," Nebala said forcefully.

"I think it really would be better," my father insisted.

"No, not by yourself," Nebala said again.

Arguing with him wasn't going to do much good. I knew that. I just didn't know if my father understood.

"Dad, maybe you could take Nebala in with—"

"No!" Nebala said, cutting me off. "Not me. Take Alexandria."

"Me?"

He nodded, and turned to my father. "Alexandria will speak of what happened."

"Certainly. That would be fine . . . good . . . of course."

"Great. I'll go along."

My father started off, and I went to follow him but skidded to a stop. I turned around, bent down, and whispered in Olivia's ear, "Watch them."

She chuckled and nodded.

Just as my father was going to knock on the office door it opened. Dakota was there, and he let out a little yelp, surprised at my father's unexpected appearance right in front of his face. Then he just looked embarrassed.

My father introduced himself, and we walked into the office. Dakota closed the door behind him. I think he was relieved that it was just the two of us.

"So, Mr. Rivers," my father began.

"Please, please, Mr. Hyatt, call me Dakota."

My father smiled. "Of course, Dakota."

I knew my father was supposed to then say, "Just call me James," but he didn't. He was establishing the hierarchy—making it clear that he was top dog. My father was older, had bags of money, and was dressed in a suit that cost more than most people paid for a car. Not to mention his Rolex watch. That was worth another couple of cars. For most people, this would have set an intimidating tone, but I knew Dakota came from money. Maybe it would have been more intimidating if my father had been dressed like a biker . . . or a Maasai.

"Thank you for coming down so quickly," Dakota said. "We could certainly use help in resolving our situation."

"Resolving situations is how I earned my first million dollars—and the second and the third and the fourth . . ." He let the sentence tail off. "But first, I was told that we have some mutual acquaintances."

"Yes, your cousin Evan and his charming wife."

"Evan's a good egg. Never had much success in business, but a good fellow nevertheless. Just seems to coast on the old man's money . . . trust fund. I'm sure that summering in Newport, you must have run into more than a few fellows like that," my father said, and he chuckled.

Dakota gave a nervous laugh, a little smile, and nodded his head. I think my father may have hit the nail on the head. That was probably what Dakota was—some rich kid with a "hobby job" living off his father's money.

"Now, Alexandria tells me that a sticking point is that our three friends have failed to post any qualifying times."

"Exactly! It is necessary for all entrants to prove that they are qualified. It certainly wouldn't be fair to our other racers if they had to dodge around or be tripped up by hordes of unqualified runners."

"That would be a problem. So how many unqualified runners have applied?" my father asked.

"Well . . . only the three of them."

"Three could hardly be described as a horde," my father said. "But still, you do have standards. Standards that are a cut above the others'."

"Yes, yes we do."

"But we also know that there's more to it than that," my father said. He got up and perched on the edge of Dakota's desk. "Dakota, you are obviously a person of, shall we say, a certain station in life . . . a man of the world."

Dakota didn't answer, but I could see by his expression that he agreed.

"As two men of the world, we know that the issue of standards goes beyond technicalities such as race times . . . if you understand what I mean."

Dakota shrugged and gave a small nod of agreement.

"You are trying to run an event that speaks of money, success, and style."

"We are certainly trying to present and preserve those elements."

"And our three friends," my father said, gesturing to the closed door, "have many fine qualities, but they certainly do not represent, even by our generous assessment, any of those things." My father paused. "We understand."

Dakota looked relieved.

"I'm so glad you see my point."

"We do," my father said. "You're here to run a world-class marathon and not some sort of circus or sideshow. Really!" my father went on. "Did you see how they're dressed? For goodness' sake, they're wearing blankets! It's like they're here for some sort of—I don't know—almost like they're going to a . . . to a . . . "

"A costume party?" Dakota said.

"Exactly! Exactly! Obviously we see eye to eye!" my father exclaimed.

And just how any of this was helping our cause was a mystery to me. It felt like my father was on Dakota's side. I almost said something then, but I decided to keep my mouth shut. Even though I didn't know what he was up to or where he was going with this, I knew my father well enough to know that *he* knew what he was doing. He hadn't got rich by being stupid.

"And there's something even worse," my father said. "Did you see what they were wearing on their feet?"

Dakota shook his head.

"Tire-tread sandals! Can you imagine what your sponsor would say?" He gestured to a big poster advertising a famous shoe brand and a wall lined with boxes of those shoes. I hadn't noticed those. "What would their reaction be if the winning runners wore tire-tread sandals instead of these shoes?"

Dakota went a bit pale beneath his tan when my father said that.

"I . . . I . . . hadn't even thought of that."

"It's a good thing one of us did," my father said. "Business is business, after all. Any event where your sponsors aren't happy is destined to be a doomed event."

"Thank you for pointing that out to me," Dakota said, a bit uneasily. "Thank you so much."

Now I really started to question where this was all headed. My father was running them right out of the race!

"I'm sure you would have thought that through eventually," my father said.

"That's most gracious of you, Mr. Hyatt, most gracious."

"Not at all, son. You were placed in this very important position for a reason. I'm sure the organizers were most impressed with your previous experience and expertise."

"Yes. My father said he couldn't think of anybody better suited to run the event."

"Your father?" my father said.

Dakota looked as though he'd been caught saying something he hadn't meant to tell us.

"Yes, my father was one of the partnership team that provided the start-up money for this event," he explained reluctantly.

"Then obviously he and *all* the partnership team have the greatest faith in you. I'm sure you'll make your father proud." My father paused. "Especially in light of how we're going to resolve this potentially explosive and damaging situation regarding your refusal to allow our friends to participate."

Dakota now looked completely confused. Welcome to the club!

"But . . . but . . . I thought we'd agreed they couldn't run," he stammered.

"I never agreed to that. I was simply helping to explain the difficult situation. You're in a very bad situation. It would be most unfortunate if we had to sue the marathon."

"Sue? What would you sue us for?" Dakota demanded.

"Well, for starters, breach of contract."

"We don't have a contract!"

"Yes, we do. You took the money and gave these men their registration packages." He turned to me. "You do have those packages, don't you?"

I held them up.

"And they are signed by the registration officer, are they not?" my father asked.

"Yes, he signed them," I said.

"But he wasn't *supposed* to sign them!" Dakota protested.

"But he *did*, and he is your sanctioned employee, so what he does is in the name of the marathon," my father said. "Money was taken and a product provided. That is a fully executed contract."

"But that can't be right."

"It is. Please feel free to contact your lawyer . . . or your father. In fact, you might want to do that immediately, because I'm going to be contacting my lawyer to ask him to go before the courts to request an injunction to stop the marathon from taking place."

"An injunction?" he gasped. "I don't understand what that means."

"Basically an injunction is a temporary restraining order ensuring that while the matter is being reviewed by the courts, *nobody* will be allowed to compete. The race will not take place."

"You can't do that!" Dakota snapped.

"Oh yes, I can. Getting an injunction is a certainty." My father sounded completely confident. That didn't mean he was—only that he needed to sound that way.

"You don't really think you could win a lawsuit, do you?"

"I don't know if I can or can't," my father replied. "What I know is that I can tie the whole thing up in the courts long enough to make sure that the race is put into jeopardy. Even if I can't win, I can guarantee you a prolonged legal fight that will cost you time and a considerable amount of money."

"But surely *you* don't want to go through a lengthy trial," Dakota said.

"Me? I won't be going through anything. I have lawyers on retainer. I'll just sic them on you like little legal pit bulls. They'll enjoy going after you, and for me, the money doesn't mean anything. All that matters is making my little girl happy." He turned to me again. "Would suing him make you happy, angel?"

I smiled. "That would make me *very* happy, Daddy."

"Then that's that." He pulled out his cellphone. "I'll call my lawyer and—"

"No!" Dakota screamed as he practically jumped across the table. "Perhaps we can discuss this further."

"I'm afraid the only discussion I'm going to be having is with the newspapers and TV networks."

"What?"

"We're not just going to fight this in the courts; we'll be taking it to the court of public opinion. I want the world to know that you consider people who are wearing traditional Kenyan tribal dress as being like part of some sort of sideshow or circus ... or what was that term you used? Yes, like people going to a *costume* party. That will certainly get people's attention, especially the other runners. Aren't the best marathon runners in the world from Kenya?"

He nodded his head slightly. His mouth was open, and there was a stunned, shocked look in his eyes.

"When they've heard that you've been insulting their countrymen I'm sure they'll withdraw from the race, leaving you a definite cut *below* the rest in terms of race competitors."

Dakota looked like a trapped animal. He didn't see any way out.

"It's all so ... so unfortunate that we have to go this route," my father said. "Although there is that one other choice."

"Other choice?" Dakota squeaked.

"Yes. It's so simple. Let them run. They are qualified."

"They are?" Dakota asked.

"Alexandria, what was that story you told me about a lion?" he asked.

"Yes, of course. Samuel once ran after a wounded lion, tracking it for days, never stopping. He ran at least sixty miles."

"Which I believe is more than two marathons, is it not?" my father asked.

"Almost two and a half," Dakota admitted.

"Then they are certainly qualified to run, wouldn't you agree?"

Dakota nodded.

"And you are allowing them to compete, correct?"

Again Dakota nodded. He knew he had no choice.

"That is excellent. Of course, that does still leave you with one little problem."

"It does?"

"Yes. What will your sponsor think if the three men wearing tire treads win the marathon they're sponsoring? They won't be happy."

"Not at all."

My father got up from his chair, circled around the desk, and put a hand on Dakota's shoulder. "You know, son, I like you. I really do. And that's why I'm going to make sure that embarrassment doesn't happen."

"You are? How?"

"I'm going to make sure they run this race in your sponsor's shoes."

"You will?"

"Of course. I'm assuming that you'll give them all shoes."

I almost laughed. I couldn't believe my father's nerve. First he'd won the fight, and now he was going to add insult to injury.

Dakota let out a big sigh. "Do you know their sizes?"

"I'm not even sure if they know their sizes," my father said. "But we'll send them in, and I'm sure you can help them find just the right shoes."

My father slapped Dakota on the back. "It's always best when we can resolve a situation so that everybody wins, and this is one of those cases!" he trumpeted.

"Yes . . . yes, it is," Dakota agreed.

Personally, I couldn't see any way that Dakota had won, other than that he'd been allowed the illusion he hadn't been beaten into the ground.

My father and I started to walk out of the office.

"Wait!" Dakota called out.

This had all seemed too easy—what now?

"If you give me an address I'll arrange to have their chips delivered—the electronic chips that they wear in the race."

"Chips?" my father asked. I was a little confused about that too.

"Each runner has an electronic chip that shows his progress throughout the route to prove that he ran the whole race."

"Are you questioning their integrity?" my father demanded.

"No, of course not!" Dakota exclaimed. "All runners have chips—it's just protocol for everybody!"

"Well . . . then, thank you," my father said. "Very considerate of you to have them delivered."

We walked out and closed the door behind us.

"Well?" my father said to me out of the corner of his mouth.

"Thank you! Thank you so much!"

"No problem. It was my pleasure."

I looked over at him. He was beaming. "You really did enjoy that, didn't you?"

"Yes, yes I did," he admitted. "And you?"

I shrugged. "It was sort of interesting to watch, although you certainly had me confused for a while there."

"You? Think about poor little Dakota!"

I laughed. "He did kind of get that deer-in-the-car-headlights look."

"Not a car. A transport truck. I wanted him to see nothing but grille coming at him."

"Remind me not to get on your bad side," I said.

"You, my angel, could *never* be on my bad side." He looked at his watch. "Now, I've got to get back to the office—call if there are any more issues."

CHAPTER FOURTEEN

I knocked on the door of the guest house, careful to keep things from sliding off the tray. The three glasses of orange juice sloshed slightly but didn't spill onto the toast or cereal sitting alongside them.

There was no answer and no noise from inside. They couldn't still be asleep, could they? No, that made no sense. Maasai always got up when the sun rose, and it was almost ten now. Then again, they were probably still on Kenyan time, which was ten hours different, so it wasn't ten in the morning it was really— No, wait ... it was ten hours *earlier* in Kenya, so for them it was more like midnight instead of ten in the morning. They had to be awake.

I knocked louder. The door shook, and this time the juice did slosh out of the glasses and onto the tray and the toast, sparing the cereal. So much for my future as a waitress. Like *that* could *ever* happen. There was still no answer, though.

I turned the knob. The door was unlocked and I pushed it open.

"Hello!" I yelled out.

There was no response to my call. I looked around. I couldn't see anybody. I slipped inside and put the tray down on the little end table.

"Nebala—guys—are you here?"

The door to the bedroom was open. There was nobody there, but the bed was made. Actually, it looked more as though it had never been slept in. Then I noticed that there were blankets on the floor, and the cushions from the living room. They'd slept on the floor. That was very Maasai. But the question wasn't where had they slept, but where were they right now. Maybe they were somewhere out on the grounds of the property.

I went outside and circled around the pool house, coming back to the front of the house. The driveway curved around the front of the property, from the gate and the high wall that surrounded the whole place, right past the house and to the garage—the *five*-car garage, my father always made a point of saying. The whole property was nothing short of immaculate—beds filled with exotic flowers, perfectly pruned shrubs, and grass so green and manicured you'd think it was artificial. It was like a work of art.

Speaking of which—where was the artist? Where was our gardener, Carlos? No Carlos and no Maasai. I had the strangest thought that the Mexican gardener had taken the Maasai out for a breakfast burrito.

I tipped back my head. What was that smell? Was it smoke? Yes, smoke . . . it was smoke. Was somebody having a barbeque, or was it from a fireplace? No, neither made any sense at ten in the morning, but there was definitely the odour of smoke, and it wasn't a particularly nice smell.

I walked toward the garage. It blocked the only part of the front of the property that I couldn't see. And as I walked, the smell of the smoke got stronger and more pungent. No barbeque. No fireplace. Not unless somebody was burning garbage in their fireplace, or— I stopped dead in my tracks. There was a wisp of black smoke rising into the air from behind the garage!

I ran toward the garage at full speed, tripping over the curb, and circling around and then skidding to a stop in disbelief. Nebala and Koyati were squatting on the ground beside a little fire that Nebala was poking with a stick.

"What are you doing?" I exclaimed.

They both gave me a look like I was crazy, like I didn't know what a fire was.

"Yes, yes, I know it's *moto*," I said, using the Swahili word for "fire," "but why have you made *moto*?"

"*Mpishi*," Nebala said.

"*Mpishi*?" That word sounded familiar. Wait . . . I knew what it meant. "But you don't have to cook anything. Carmella made you breakfast . . . well, really more like brunch."

"Brunch?" Nebala questioned. "What type of animal is brunch?"

I laughed. "Brunch isn't an animal; it's a meal. Sort of half breakfast and half lunch—brunch. I have it waiting for you in the guest house . . ."

I suddenly realized that I'd been so startled by the fire that I hadn't even thought of the fact that there was one Maasai missing.

"Where's Samuel?" I asked.

Nebala gestured to the wall surrounding our property.

"He climbed over the wall?"

He nodded.

The wall separated our property from our neighbours'. I really hadn't ever said much to our neighbours—a high wall generally discourages conversation—but I did know that they had a guard at their gate and all sorts of high-tech security cameras ringing the street. I figured that meant they weren't going to be happy to have *any* stranger waltzing through their property, and quite frankly, I had trouble even imagining an intruder who would be stranger than Samuel . . . well, except for Koyati or Nebala.

"He shouldn't be over there!" I exclaimed. "We have to get him back."

"He will be back soon," Nebala said.

"Soon isn't good enough. Why is he even over there to begin with?"

"Looking for food," he said. "Hunting."

"There's lots of food in the kitchen and— Hunting? What do you mean hunting?" I gasped.

"Looking for food. He took a bow and arrow and—"

"A bow and arrow? Where did he get a bow and arrow?"

"We made them from the tree." He pointed to one of our very expensive shrubs.

I could see where they had hacked away some branches. Carlos was going to be furious! I had a vision of a battle between one angry Mexican armed with a leaf-blower and three Maasai with *kongas* . . . and now at least one bow and arrow. That would be one strange pay-for-view cage match, one bizarre reality TV show, and— Again, that wasn't the issue.

Samuel had a bow and arrow, he was on my neighbours' property, and he was hunting!

"We have to stop him!" I screamed out. "How did he get over the wall?"

"He climbed."

"I have to get over there."

"You want to go hunting?" Nebala asked.

"No!" I exclaimed. "I have to stop Samuel from hunting!"

I ran over to the wall. It was solid stone and close to ten feet high. It was smooth, with no place to grab hold to pull myself up. I raised my hand. The top was well above my reach. How had he managed to climb over this? I needed help.

"Don't just stand there!" I yelled. "Give me a boost!"

Both men jumped to their feet. I was almost startled by their quick reaction.

"Lift me up!" I put my hands together to show them how to do it, and they instantly mimicked me.

I put my foot in and— "Aaaah!" They threw me up into the air! I landed on the top of the wall, partially knocking my breath out. I teetered precariously on the edge, struggling to regain my balance. It was a long way down in either direction.

I pulled myself up so I had a leg on each side of the wall to steady me and looked into my neighbours' yard. If I could see Samuel I could just yell for him to come back. But I didn't see him. The property was big—even bigger than our estate—but rather than being open it was filled with a tangle of trees and shrubs and bushes. I couldn't see Samuel. I couldn't see very far at all. Maybe I could scream for him—no, I couldn't do that. I couldn't guarantee that the people in the house or at the security gate wouldn't hear. I had to go down onto their property. Easier said than done.

I looked along the wall. Not too far off to my right there were trees that were almost right against the wall, with branches going almost over the top. Then I remembered why those branches went "almost" over the wall. My father had complained about how they were "littering" our property with leaves that were getting in our pool. He'd spoken to our neighbours, and when nothing happened he had Carlos cut off anything that extended over the fence and over our property. They complained—sent a letter from their lawyer and threatened to sue us. Nothing unusual there—sometimes I thought suing people was almost like a hobby in this country—but nothing more ever came of it.

That was probably five years ago, and they hadn't spoken to us since. If my father hadn't wanted their leaves in his garden I could only imagine how happy they'd be about having his *daughter* in theirs. Best thing was not to let them know that I was there.

I scuttled along the top of the wall. This was working, but it was working slowly—and this couldn't be good for my Capri pants. They were far too nice and expensive to be scraped or snagged. There had to be a faster way, and a way that wouldn't damage my wardrobe.

The wall was about eight inches wide, smooth and straight—like a balance beam. It was time for all those years of gymnastics to pay off.

Slowly I rose to my feet, my arms extended for balance, until I was standing. Foot over foot I moved, slowly, but it was much faster and more dignified than dragging my bottom along the wall. I stopped and took hold of one of the branches, grabbing it with my hands to test its strength. It moved, but it seemed strong enough to hold me. This would be my way down—and my way back up.

I swung one leg over the branch. It sank down lower to allow me on and I put my entire weight on it, causing it to come right down to the top of the wall. It actually now extended over the wall. Good thing my father couldn't see that or there would be another order for Carlos and his chainsaw to roar into action.

I inched my way down the branch until I came to the trunk. From there I lowered myself the rest of the way and dropped silently to the ground. Anxiously I looked all around. I couldn't see Samuel, but I could see that this was more than just a jungle. From my perch on the wall the branches and leaves had hidden the manicured paths that cut between the trees. There were little decorative ponds that were filled with koi, like big, fat goldfish—big, fat, expensive goldfish. Some of those could have been worth hundreds of dollars . . . Was Samuel thinking about a fish fry for breakfast?

I moved among the trees. It was good to have so much to hide behind, but at the same time, not so good, because I couldn't see Samuel . . . or anybody else who might be there. I kept moving along.

"Samuel!" I called out quietly, wanting to be heard but at the same time, not.

There was no reply. It felt as if my voice was being absorbed by all the trees. I kept moving forward until I could start to make out the house. I stopped at the edge of the trees. There was a lawn—long and lush and well manicured—and beyond that the home. It was big, made of a pinkish sandstone. It struck me as a little bit tacky. Pink was my favourite colour, but really it looked like some sort of overblown version of Barbie's Dream House. I wondered if they had Barbie's Dream Corvette parked in the garage.

There was a cat out on the lawn—a beautiful Siamese cat. Did Barbie have a cat? It had just come out of the trees and was slowly walking across the grass toward the house. I'm not really a "cat person," but if I were to have a cat it would be something like that—something exotic, perhaps a Siamese, or even one of those hairless cats, those Sphynx cats. I'd only seen one or two of them myself. They certainly got people's attention. Not that my dog, Sprout, would *ever* allow a cat in his home.

The cat continued to move across the grass at a leisurely pace. Cats certainly have a sense of style. You could almost picture this one as a high-priced, high-strung, high-fashion model on the runway. The big difference would be that cats only throw up hairballs and not their— My attention was caught by motion in the trees just to my right. It was Samuel!

Thank goodness I'd found him. Now we could go back. . . . Wait . . . what was he doing? He was crouched down and he had his bow and arrow out—and he was aiming for the cat! The bow arched as he pulled back the string and—

"Samuel!" I screamed.

He started, and the arrow flew and stuck into the ground—so close that it startled the cat, which bolted away!

Samuel looked at me with disbelief. He jumped to his feet and ran onto the lawn, chasing his prey.

"No!" I screamed as I ran out of the trees after him.

He skidded to a stop and pulled his arrow out of the grass. I caught up to him and grabbed him by the arm. I shocked both of us when I pulled him to his feet.

"We have to go! Right now!" I yelled into his face. "We have to—"

My words were erased by the wail of a siren screaming out an alarm!

CHAPTER FIFTEEN

I stumbled forward, pulling Samuel with me down the path and toward the tree that would help us over the wall. The wail of the alarm chased after us, the sound muffled by the trees but still loud and ominous.

"This way," I said. "Just follow me."

We raced along the path. My feet thumped loudly against the stones while Samuel's made no sound. We reached the wall, and I bent over to catch my breath. I looked at Samuel. He smiled. He wasn't winded at all.

"All we have to do is climb the tree . . ." I wasn't sure which tree. There were a bunch close to the wall and their branches reached up and intermingled, so I wasn't sure which branches came from which tree. Picking the wrong tree might mean not getting over the wall and getting caught. Picking *no* tree meant *not* getting over the wall and getting caught. Better to die trying.

"This one, I think. Let's go up this one."

I didn't know if this was the tree I'd come in on, but it was the one I was going to try to use to leave. I jumped up and grabbed the fork of the tree, pulling myself up. I went up to the first branch while Samuel jumped and pulled himself up into the tree right behind me. I moved from branch to branch. I was even impressing myself with how fast I was moving. Fear was a pretty strong motivator. There was a branch leading up to and above the wall. It wasn't that thick, but it was certainly thick enough to hold me . . . wasn't it?

I started shimmying along the branch, upside down. I could feel it sagging under my weight. Maybe this wasn't such a good idea, but there was no way back now. I climbed farther and farther until I bumped my head into the wall. I looked backwards and then spiralled around, reaching up and out until I had my hand on the top of the wall. I pulled myself up, twisting around until I plopped down, right on top! I'd made it!

In the distance I could hear voices—loud voices. Somebody was coming after us!

"Come on!" I called out to Samuel, who was still standing in the lower branches of the tree. Was he afraid of climbing higher? Was he afraid of heights? No, that didn't make any sense because he had a huge smile on his face. Did he find everything amusing? This was no time to be amused! Didn't he realize how much trouble we could be in?

"You've got to get over here!"

He nodded his head and amazingly his smile grew even larger. He started scampering up the tree, practically bouncing from branch to branch until he came to the one I'd used to reach the wall. He stepped on the branch and started to walk along it! He was moving along the branch as if it were a tightrope—no, not a tightrope; he didn't even have his arms out to balance himself. It was more like he was strolling along the sidewalk. He took a few more steps and then leaped, flying through the air and landing on top of the wall! He wobbled a little bit and then regained his equilibrium and stood straight up.

The voices seemed to be getting louder, which meant they were getting closer, and I was still—technically—on my neighbours' property because one of my legs was dangling over their side. I swung my leg over and started to lower myself down onto my own property. My fingers started to give way and I tumbled down, hitting the bottom and then rolling over, almost doing a back somersault.

I rolled back to a seated position. Samuel stood way above me, and he was doubled over and laughing. Glad I could add a little joy to his life.

"Get down here!" I yelled. "Now . . . *sasa*! Quickly . . . *epesi*!"

He jumped off the wall, hit the ground, rolled onto his side, and then, in one motion, sprang back to his feet! It was like some sort of special-effects thing from a karate movie, except he didn't have any wires attached. But we were safely on our side of the wall, and he'd done it just in time because the voices were even louder now . . . and coming from *behind* me. How was that possible?

I turned around. Nebala and Koyati and Carlos were

all standing around the smouldering remains of the fire, yelling at one another, gesturing madly with their hands. I got to my feet and ran over. They continued to scream at one another—Carlos in Spanish, and Nebala and Koyati in a combination of Maa and Swahili. I understood a smattering of the words they were saying but knew that none of them had *any* idea what was being yelled at them—although they certainly had a pretty good idea what was being communicated non-verbally.

"All of you stop!" I screamed as I stepped between them, but nobody did.

Instead they all began yelling louder, the words coming more quickly so they all seemed to blur together. It sounded as if they were speaking Spanhili, or maybe Swalish, and I couldn't make out anything that was being screamed.

"*Silencio! Usu!*" They all continued to ignore me and went on yelling.

"Could you at least all yell in English?" I demanded. "Then I could figure out what you're all so mad about!"

The yelling match suddenly, surprisingly, stopped. Carlos looked as though he wanted to talk but the words just wouldn't come out in English. He was so angry that he'd lost a whole language. His face got redder and redder and his eyes bugged out and—

"My tree!" he screamed. "They hacked up my tree, my *beeeautiful* tree!"

"Technically, it's *my* tree," I said.

He now looked shocked. "*Your* tree?"

"Yes, if you think about it, all the trees are mine . . . well, at least they belong to my family."

"You? Your family? When was the last time I saw you out here pruning? When was the last time your mother sprayed for aphids or your father fertilized?" he demanded. "This tree, she is *my* tree! Those flowers . . . they are *my* flowers! These bushes are *my* bushes!" he yelled, gesturing around as he spoke. He was still angry, but now he seemed to be angry at me. I had never seen him that mad before—actually, I'd never seen him *mad* before.

"Do you remember when this tree was sick?" he demanded.

I didn't, but I nodded my head.

"I nursed her back to health. Do you think I did that so some . . . some . . . *people* could hurt her, could cause her pain?"

Nebala didn't look happy. He barked out some words and Samuel came forward. He took the bow from his back and removed the two arrows from his belt—he was going to shoot Carlos!

"No, no, you can't do that!" I yelled as I jumped in front of our gardener to protect him. He didn't have a leaf-blower to use in his defence.

Samuel handed the bow and arrow to Nebala. Nebala then took a step forward, extending his hands, holding the weapons out to Carlos.

"We did not know it was your tree. We return what we took without asking." He bowed his head slightly.

"I don't want your bow!" Carlos said. "Just . . . just don't do that again . . . okay?"

Nebala nodded. "We took what was not ours to

take. We offer our apology." He extended his hands farther, offering the bow and arrow again.

I knew it would be an insult if Carlos didn't take them.

"Please, Carlos . . . it's an apology," I explained.

Reluctantly Carlos took the bow and arrow from him and then looked at the offering. "Your apology is accepted." He reached out his other hand and the two men shook. He then did the same with Samuel and Koyati.

"That's better," I said, sighing in relief. "They just didn't know it was a special tree."

"All trees are special," Nebala said.

"That's right!" Carlos exclaimed. "Each and every one."

Nebala nodded in agreement. "Each plant, each tree, each rock has its own spirit."

"I don't know about the rock part, but I agree with the part about plants," Carlos said.

"And all of this," Nebala said, gesturing around the yard, "is yours?"

"All of it."

"These plants are all strange to us. Where we live we know each plant, each tree, each rock, each clump of dirt. Is that how you know these plants?"

"I know them like I know my own family members."

"Yes, yes, because they are like family—each has a spirit," Nebala said. "You must have great knowledge."

Carlos actually puffed out his chest. "Thank you."

"Could we ask of you a great favour?" Nebala asked. "Could you teach us?"

"I could teach you a thing or two."

"We wish to know which of these would be used for medicine," Nebala said.

I laughed. "We get our medicine from the pharma—"

"Shows what she knows!" Carlos said, cutting me off. "There are plants here that can be used for indigestion, rashes, to make your skin soft, and to heal infections."

"Really?" I gasped.

"Really, yes."

"And food, which of these plants are foul and which are for food?"

I almost said something but didn't want to look stupid again.

"Most of this stuff is just to look at," Carlos said.

"Not to eat?"

"Decorative. Eye candy. Do you know how much food could be grown on a piece of land this size? People here seem to think that it is better to look good than to be good!" he exclaimed.

"So none of this is for food?" Nebala asked. I didn't know whether he sounded sad or confused, or both.

"Well, I can show you leaves that can be made into tea, some roots that can be cooked to make a good stew, and some herbs to make that stew taste spicy."

"I didn't know any of that," I said.

He huffed. "You cannot learn everything watching that NTV!"

"It's MTV, and I do go to school."

"There are things you cannot learn in school, only through life or—"

"Excuse me!" came a voice.

We turned toward the back door of the house. It was Carmella.

"Alexandria, there are some men at the gate wishing to come in," she said.

"Men? What sort of men, and why do they want in?"

"*Policia*," she said. "And they wish to talk to somebody about trying to kill a cat and trespassing. I tell them we know nothing . . . Is that right?"

I gulped. Maybe that wasn't right, but I certainly didn't want to tell them anything different. Maybe we could explain all this to the cranky neighbours, but maybe it would end up with Samuel being hauled into court, charges being pressed, and Samuel missing the race. I couldn't let that happen—too much was riding on it. I figured this was one of those times when bending the truth to help somebody else might be the right thing to do. After all, it was a victimless crime—even the cat got away safely!

"Is my mother home?" I asked.

"No, she leave."

"Good. Go back and let them in."

She turned to leave.

"But, Carmella, please take your time. We need to get ready for their arrival."

CHAPTER SIXTEEN

I stood outside the front door and watched as the big gate opened up and the police car entered and came slowly up the driveway toward me. It came to a stop right in front of me, in front of the house, and two officers climbed out.

They were both young and tanned, with perfect hair and capped teeth, and they wore designer shades. Even the police officers in L.A. looked like movie stars. Was there some sort of bylaw that you couldn't live or work here if you weren't at least fashion-friendly?

"Good morning," one of the officers—the slightly younger one—said.

"Good morning," I replied, trying my best to sound friendly—friendly and innocent. I was innocent until proven guilty, and as long as the three Maasai stayed hidden in the wine cellar where Carmella had placed them, I'd *stay* innocent.

"We've had a complaint," the one officer said.

"That's too bad, but my father always says there's no point in complaining about anything because nobody really—"

"No," he said. "Not complaining, a *complaint.*"

"Oh . . . what does that mean?" I asked, trying to sound dumb to go along with the innocent act.

"It means that we received a phone call from your neighbours about a disturbance."

"My neighbours are disturbed? Is that dangerous? Should you be calling somebody, like a psychiatrist or—?"

"No, no. Not *disturbed* . . . disturbance," he said. "They made a complaint about—"

"They should take my father's advice about not complaining, because nobody wants to hear about what you think is wrong. It's better just to have a happy outlook on life!" I said, adding an element of kooky cheerfulness to go along with dumb and innocent.

The one officer let out a big sigh. Maybe I could get them so frustrated they'd just leave.

He took a deep breath. "Look, let me try to explain it one more—"

"Let me try it," the other officer said, putting a hand on the first one's shoulder. He was just a little more perfect than his partner, and that somehow made him *less* handsome. Even perfection needed a fault. I looked at the name tag on his chest—Officer Owen Osler—perfect alliteration, but it sounded more like the name of a character on a police show than a real police officer.

The first officer bowed from the waist. "Certainly. Be my guest."

"Your neighbour called because he said there was a trespasser in his yard."

"Then shouldn't you be there catching the trespasser rather than here asking me questions?" I asked.

"They reported that the trespasser climbed *out* of their enclosure and *into* yours," Officer Osler explained.

"You think there might be an intruder here?" I glanced around anxiously. Next step in the evolution—add in a dash of worried, just bordering on paranoia. "Should I be scared? Is he dangerous? Should I call the po—Wait, you *are* here. Thank goodness!"

"I'm sure there's nothing to worry about."

"If there isn't, why are you here?"

"We have to investigate. Standard operating procedure."

"Which wall did he climb over, and when did it happen?"

"Less than twenty minutes ago. The wall behind your garage."

Just beside the garage, Carlos was working in one of the flower beds. He knew the parts we were going to play—we'd worked it out before the police arrived.

"Our gardener has been working over there all morning. If anybody came over the wall I'm sure he would have noticed. I'll call him over." I took a few steps in his direction. "Carlos!" I yelled. "Come . . . *venga!*"

He looked up, stood up, and leaned on his shovel.

"*Rapidamente!*" I yelled, and he started walking.

"You speak some Spanish," one of the officers said.

"Oh, just a little bit," I replied. "In southern California it's almost impossible to get by without some Spanish, especially since so many of these people learn so little English."

Carlos came over and removed his hat.

"Carlos, these are police officers . . . they are not from immigration," I said, saying each word loudly and slowly and clearly. I turned to the officers. "You know how they're always afraid you're going to pick them up and ship them south of the border. Even when they've already got their cards, like Carlos, they still worry.

"Carlos, have you seen any . . . any . . ." I turned back to the officers. "I don't know the Spanish word for 'trespassers.'"

"I do," the first officer said.

He quickly spat out a question to Carlos. I knew enough to figure out what he'd asked. Carlos was going to deny seeing anybody. He shook his head no and then proceeded, in Spanish, to tell him he'd been working in the yard all day and he would have seen somebody climbing the wall, but he'd seen nobody.

"Well, that's settled," I said. "He didn't see anybody."

The officer gave me a confused look. "I thought you didn't speak that much Spanish."

I started slightly, then recovered my composure. "I understand more than I speak," I said. "Besides, I certainly understand what it means when somebody shakes his head—unless that means 'yes' in Spanish." I wanted to change the subject. "Did the neighbours tell you what this intruder looked like?"

"That's the strange part," the officer said. "They said there were two intruders. One of them was described as looking like an African warrior, all dressed in red, and he was carrying a bow and arrow, which he used to try to shoot their prized Siamese cat."

"The neighbours on this side?" I asked, pointing to the wall in the direction we all knew. "You have to know that they have a little problem." I held my thumb to my mouth and tipped back my hand and head. "A little bit of a drinking problem . . . not that I like to gossip." I paused. "I didn't even know they had a cat. Perhaps it's a sign of age. They are getting a bit older . . . perhaps their eyes are starting to go a little."

"Really? Interesting that they described the second intruder as being a young girl with blonde hair, about your age, and wearing clothes that exactly match your clothing."

I laughed. "In southern California it's almost impossible to find a woman who *isn't* blonde, *isn't* dressed fashionably, and doesn't at least *look* my age from a distance—even women in their sixties. I guess that's the beauty of cosmetic surgery. Everybody can look young . . . at least from a distance. How close did these people get to this supposed intruder?"

"Probably not close enough to get a good look at her face, if that's what you're worried about, Alexandria," the officer said.

"I'm not worried about anything," I said, "because I have nothing to be worried about, and— How do you know my name? I didn't tell you my name . . . did I?"

"The beauty of modern police work," the one officer said. "We ran the address on the computer in our car and found the names of all people living at this residence."

"All people and all their previous criminal convictions," the other officer added.

Okay, innocent had gone out the window.

"And we were able to discover that you have three previous convictions as a juvenile."

"Three?"

"Three," he said, holding up three fingers as a little visual. "Vandalism, theft under, and then a breach-of-probation charge."

"That's really only two . . . Two little misunderstandings from when I was a kid."

"Those offences were within the last year."

"That was so long ago. I've changed . . . especially since I've—" I stopped myself before I could finish the sentence and tell them about all the charity work I was doing to help people in Africa . . . the place where African warriors with bows and arrows came from.

"Since what?" the officer asked.

"Since . . . since . . . I've turned sixteen. I've learned my lesson. I've matured, grown up, taken responsibility."

"Have you?" he asked.

The tone of his voice left little question that he doubted me. I had to do something to remove that doubt.

"If you'd like, you have my permission to search my house and the entire property. You don't even need a search warrant." I thought I'd offer a little bluff.

"So you're saying you'll let us search the entire house and the grounds," he said.

Was he was trying to call my bluff?

"Of course," I answered. I didn't blink. "I'd love to clear this up."

The two officers looked at each other, and then one shrugged.

"I guess that won't be necessary."

I'd won the bluff. But I did have a backup plan. I'd watched enough episodes of *Law & Order* to know that they really *did* need a warrant if they wanted to search, so if they tried to take me up on my offer I'd just take it back. By the time they did get back with a warrant—if they even bothered—my Maasai would be safely hidden somewhere else, maybe at Olivia's house.

"I'd actually *want* you to search if the whole thing weren't so silly," I said.

"There's nothing silly about a trespassing charge, especially for somebody with previous criminal convictions. It could be very serious," the second officer said.

"I mean the *whole* thing. Can you really believe that there was a Maasai warrior in my neighbours' yard who was trying to kill a cat for breakfast? That's just too silly to—"

"Who said anything about breakfast?" Officer Osler asked.

"And who mentioned Maasai warriors specifically?" the other officer questioned.

I felt a flush creep over my whole body. I couldn't even choke out an attempt at a lie.

"What school do you go to?" Officer Osler asked.

"Beverly Hills High."

"Grade?"

"Eleven."

"You know that this is really more like a village than a city," Officer Osler said. "And my nephew, he's in grade eleven at your school."

"Maybe I know him," I offered, looking for any connection that might get me out of this. Often life simply revolved around who you knew.

"It's a big school," he said, "and I doubt he runs with *your* crowd."

I didn't like the way he said "your crowd," like it was a bad thing. Great, I was going to be in trouble because I had money. At least it wasn't like I'd rejected his nephew, because I didn't even know who he was.

"Well, my nephew was telling me about a girl in his school who had been to Africa and was now raising money to help needy people. Have you heard anything about that?"

"It does sound familiar," I said.

"And I do believe he even mentioned that her name was Alexandria."

"That's such a common name in my school," I said, flashing my sweetest, most innocent smile. "I wish my parents had tried something a little more imaginative."

The policeman pulled a cellphone out of his pocket. "Maybe I should call my nephew and ask him the name of this wonderful young lady who is trying to help the disadvantaged."

That sick feeling in my stomach got worse. I was as good as caught. I could just see myself going back before the court, before that judge, once again, except this time there'd be no way out of me having to live in a little cell and wear an orange jumpsuit. God, I looked awful in orange! The only things that did look good in orange were pylons and certain citrus fruits.

He looked me directly in the eyes. "Do you think I should make that phone call?" he asked.

I shook my head.

"I didn't think so." He paused. "My nephew also told me that this girl, Alexandria Something-or-other, used to be a royal pain, that she acted like she owned the school and was rude and rather obnoxious and spoiled. You know the type."

I didn't answer, but obviously even if I didn't know his nephew he knew me—or at least knew who I used to be. It was hard to break a reputation once it had been made.

"And just out of curiosity, if we do catch that girl who was trespassing, what do you think we should do with her?"

I shrugged and shook my head again. Now he was toying with me. Why not just arrest me and get it over with?

"I have a question for you," the officer said. "That girl who was over on her neighbours' property, do you think she was trying to do anything wrong?"

"No!" I exclaimed. "She was trying to *stop* something

wrong from happening ... at least, that's what I think she must have been doing."

"I think so too," Officer Osler said. "And not that I'm asking you if you were over there, because I'm not, but if you were on your neighbours' property, you wouldn't be going over there again, would you?"

"No, never. Honestly."

"That's good to know, because I'd hate to be the one to arrest somebody who's trying to do the right thing. Sometimes the hardest disadvantage to over-come is a lack of disadvantage," he said.

"What?" I questioned.

"All this," he said, gesturing around the property, "makes it harder for a person who has so much to understand those who have so little. It takes a remark-able person to rise above her upbringing to become a caring person. I'm not going to be the one to arrest that person."

"So I think we should maybe go now," the other officer said. "And I'm sure that whatever *didn't* happen here *won't* happen again."

They opened up their car doors and started to climb in.

"Wait!" I called out. "Is that it?"

"Do you want there to be something else?"

"No, I'm happy ... thanks."

"That's okay. We all agree that nothing happened here, right?" he asked.

"Yes, nothing happened," I agreed. "And you have my word that the nothing that happened won't happen again."

"I know that. Take care."

He climbed into the car and they drove away, leaving Carlos and me standing there watching them as they disappeared through the gate.

Carlos starting chuckling.

"What's so funny?"

"Just think, the *policia* came, and they left the Mexican alone and almost arrested the rich white girl. Pretty funny, no?"

"Not that funny."

"You are a pretty good liar," Carlos said.

"I would prefer to consider it more in the nature of a dramatic performance."

"Then you are very good at drama . . . like a drama *queen*."

"I'll take that as a compliment. You didn't do so bad yourself."

He shrugged. "I am a pretty good drama queen too. I am going back to my gardening." He started to walk away, then stopped. "They will not be making any more bows, will they?"

"I think I can promise you that won't happen again."

"*Bueno.*"

"*Mucho bueno.*"

CHAPTER SEVENTEEN

I couldn't believe that I'd slept in as late as I had. It was almost eleven. I guess all the drama of the last few days had taken more out of me than I'd thought. I wandered downstairs, still wearing my jammies and fluffy slippers. The whole house was quiet. I walked into the dining room—the table had been set for four, and there were now three plates showing evidence of three people having eaten breakfast. That was good. They'd eaten in here, eaten what Carmella had prepared, rather than going out in search of our neighbours' pets. We'd come to an agreement that pets and plants were all off limits, and that Carmella would make them any food they wanted.

Speaking of which, I was kind of hoping she'd make *me* some food. Carmella made just about the best

Spanish omelettes in the world, although she called them Mexican omelettes. Either way, they were pretty wonderful.

I had started to wander toward the kitchen when my attention was caught by a flash of red through the window. I went over and peered out. It was Nebala standing in a flower bed with Carlos, and they seemed to be talking. I guessed Carlos was giving him gardening hints, or maybe explaining what he could have for dessert after breakfast.

At least I knew where one of my Maasai was. Unfortunately, it was the other two who worried me more. I was sure they couldn't be too far away, and I was sure that Nebala would know where they were. Breakfast would go down more easily once I knew where all three of them were. I didn't want to take any chances of a repeat visit from our friendly neighbourhood police department.

I went outside in my slippers and scuffled over to the flower bed. The two men were so occupied with their conversation that they didn't even notice my arrival. I never liked it when I wasn't noticed.

"Good morning!" I said loudly.

They looked over, and while they both nodded they continued with their conversation. Nebala was holding some flower bulbs. They were dirty and looked as though they'd just been dug up.

"No, no!" Carlos said emphatically. "These are not for eating, just for looking."

"Looking for what?" Nebala asked.

"Not looking for anything, but for seeing—you

know, like . . . like a treat for your eyes because they are so *beeeeautiful.*"

Nebala brought the bulbs right up to his eyes and shook his head. "Still not so beautiful."

"Not now!" Carlos exclaimed. "When they become flowers. These bulbs become most *beeeeautiful* flowers."

"You can't eat flowers," Nebala said. "Maize is beautiful. Cassava is beautiful. Even rice and potatoes are beautiful."

"Maize *is* beautiful," Carlos agreed. "It would be good to grow real food here instead of just things to look at."

"You could plant some vegetables here if you wanted," I offered.

"Here?" Carlos sounded as though he didn't believe me.

"Well, not right here in front of the house, but I'm sure nobody would object if you planted a vegetable garden behind the garage or around the side of the house."

"Really?"

"Really. I'll talk to my mother . . . Do you know where she is? Have you seen her?"

"She's doing yoga in her special place," Carlos said.

Her special place was a Zen garden. It had ornamental shrubs and trellises, hanging plants, and a little reflective pond with a trickle of water running down some rocks. There were wind chimes hanging from the trees that gently sounded in the breeze. And of course, there was a little brass Buddha in the middle. I liked that Buddha. He had a knowing little smile, as though he was in possession of an important secret, a really important secret . . . or maybe he'd heard a good joke.

I had to hand it to my mother. When she got into something she really got into it completely. If she ever decided she liked go-karts we'd have a full track running around the property.

"And where are Samuel and Koyati?" I asked.

"With your mother."

"They're watching her do yoga?"

"No, no," Carlos said. "They are yogaing too."

"They're doing yoga?"

"*Si.*"

"Oh, this I have to see! Excuse me."

I walked across the property and toward the garden. Getting closer, I could hear the gentle strains of music playing—pan flutes and sitars. Why did yoga music always have pan flutes or a sitar? Mixed in with the music were the gentle sounds of the wind chimes and running water.

I caught my first glance of my mother through the shrubs. She was standing, bent over at the waist, her arms dangling down so far that her wrists were draped along the ground. She really was flexible for a woman her age—I didn't even know if I could reach that far.

Next I saw Samuel and Koyati. They were mirroring my mother's movement.

"Breathe in and out . . . five breaths," my mother said. "Remember, in and out through your nose."

There was the sound of breathing as an extra layer on top of the twang of the sitar. Slowly, in and out . . .

in and out . . . in and out . . . in and out . . . in and out.

"Plank," my mother called out.

She kicked out her feet into what almost looked like a push-up position. Samuel and Koyati looked up, looked at her, and then quickly mimicked her movement.

"Feel your breath . . . slowly . . . exhale Upward-facing Dog . . . inhale Downward-facing Dog."

Each time they watched and then quickly copied what she was doing.

"Sun Salutations and Warrior One."

It wasn't Warrior One—it was two warriors!

"Bring your feet together and reach up in Sun Salutations."

They all reached up for the sky as if they were trying to touch the sun.

"Now close your eyes and breathe . . . big, deep, cleansing breaths."

I could hear them breathing loudly. They were all standing, eyes closed, arms high in the air.

"And that's where we'll end," she said.

They all opened their eyes.

"That looked like a good workout," I said.

"I'm sorry. Did you want to join us?"

"I was sleeping."

"It was very energizing," my mother offered.

"That's exactly how I find sleeping. So how did they do?"

Samuel and Koyati looked relaxed—even Koyati was smiling just a bit—so I had to assume they'd enjoyed it. I wished Nebala could have been there to translate for them—I'd have loved to know what they made of it all!

"They're naturals! They have such amazing balance and flexibility," my mother said.

"It did look like they were doing pretty well," I agreed.

"I was shocked. This was their first time, but it was as if they have been practising yoga their entire lives."

"I think their lives keep them in balance," I suggested.

"I would love to go to Africa and see how they live," my mother said.

"Really?" I asked.

"Why not?"

"It's just that you never mentioned it before . . . I didn't know you were interested."

"I've always been interested." She paused. "At least interested since you returned, and now that I've met the Maasai I'm even more interested. How about next summer?"

"That would be wonderful."

I tried to picture my mother in Kenya. If it was a shock for me, I couldn't even imagine how much bigger the shock was going to be for her. It would be fun to watch—the same way the veterans of the program I was in watched me. My mother would be struggling like a fish out of water—no, like a fish out of *Perrier*. I'd lived the Beverly Hills lifestyle for sixteen years, but my mother had been part of it for forty-five years. It would be even harder for her to adapt.

"So what's on the schedule for today?" my mother asked.

"I'm going to take the guys out for a drive along the marathon route."

"That's sounds like a wise idea. When are you going to go?" she asked.

"After school."

"Excellent. That should give me more than enough time to take the pictures I need."

"Pictures?"

"Yes. Nebala, Koyati, and Samuel have agreed that I can take pictures of them for my class assignment."

"You're taking a photography course now?"

"No, the computer course. I'm building a website. They've given me permission to do a website about them coming here to run in the marathon. Isn't that interesting?"

"It *is* pretty interesting," I agreed, a bit reluctantly. "But I don't want them disappearing into your studio for hours on end." I wasn't crazy about the idea of my mother monopolizing their time—and I knew how obsessive she could be. "I'm sure this little website idea is important to *you*, but winning the race is what's important to *them*. Nothing should get in the way of their training."

"They don't seem to do much training, do they?" she noted.

I hadn't even really thought about it. "I guess they don't feel that they need to train because they normally spend all their time training. But I'm sure they will be going out training . . . I just don't want you to get in their way."

"I'll try not to interfere . . . and I'm sure they know what they're doing," she said reassuringly.

"I'm sure," I agreed . . . although I wasn't feeling that reassured. "I'm sure there won't be any problem with you doing your little website thing. Just go ahead and do it."

CHAPTER EIGHTEEN

This was starting to feel like déjà vu all over again—
Olivia beside me; the three Maasai in the back seat;
Samuel sitting in the middle, no seatbelt, semi-standing,
pretending to fly. The only difference was that this time
I'd given up trying to tell him to sit down. He was a big
boy, and if he really wanted to fly he'd have that opportunity if I had to stop quickly. Although at the speed I
was travelling there wasn't much danger of him going
too far.

"Turn right on Santa Monica," Olivia said.

I was driving and she was navigating, keeping us
on the marathon route.

I slowed down—very gently to keep Samuel in the
car—and made the turn.

"We're going to go right by Rodeo. Maybe we should
hang a right and show it to them," I jokingly suggested.

"We're *going* to turn right," Olivia said. "The route goes right down Rodeo."

"Wow, that's impressive. But I guess that's what the whole Beverly Hills Marathon thing is about . . . trying to impress people."

"I don't think it's working on everybody," Olivia said, gesturing to our passengers.

I adjusted the rear-view mirror so I could look into the back seat. They didn't look impressed—they looked the way they always did. Nebala looked thoughtful and sort of regal. Samuel looked happy. Koyati had that scowl in place, like he was either perpetually angry or really, really badly constipated.

I turned onto Rodeo Drive. A little shiver went up my spine. Even if it didn't have an impact on them it still impressed *me*, and I'd been here thousands of times. This was, without a doubt, *the* most exclusive, expensive, elite shopping street in the entire world. It wasn't long, but it was long on money. It started at Santa Monica and ended three blocks later, at Wilshire. In that short space, basically every designer in the world had a storefront, which meant visibility. Anybody who was anybody *had* to have a location on Rodeo.

Some of the stores were so exclusive that you couldn't even just drop in and shop—you had to make an appointment. . . and they didn't let just anybody make an appointment. I guess they ran some sort of credit check to make sure you could afford to shop there. I'd heard about movie stars coming and spending about $100,000 in under an hour.

Before Africa, that would have been like a dream

come true for me—to go into one of those stores and shop until I dropped. Right after Africa it seemed like an obscene thing to do—I knew what that amount of money could have done for the people living there. Now it was almost like I was someplace in the middle. I still liked to shop and wear nice clothes, and I did live in what a lot of people would call a mansion, but I had pangs of guilt about how much I had, and believe it or not, I actually tried to restrain myself. In a lot of ways, it was easier before, when I didn't have to think about it.

Olivia turned in her seat. "What do you think?" she asked the Maasai.

"It is . . . it is . . . a nice street," Nebala offered. "The road is very smooth, and the trees and bushes are very healthy."

He was referring to the gardens that filled the median.

"I mean the stores!" Olivia exclaimed.

"They are . . . they are nice too."

"Nice? That's Christian Dior on the right, and down from that is Gucci, and across the street is Chanel, and just up ahead is Armani, and—"

"You're wasting your breath," I said. "Shopping isn't going to impress them."

"Maybe if we stopped we could show you," Olivia said. "Maybe we could even shop a little?"

"There's no time for shopping," I told her. What I didn't say was that I knew they couldn't afford to shop in any of these stores. She must have known that too.

"Where do I go from here?" I asked.

"Turn right on Sunset Boulevard." She sighed. "If Rodeo Drive doesn't impress them, I don't know if anything in the world can."

"I don't know. They might be impressed with lots of things, but they just don't show it," I suggested. "Let's ask." I adjusted the mirror again so I could see Nebala's face—which meant he could see mine.

"So what do you think of Beverly Hills?" I asked.

"Many things are very different."

"But have you seen anything that impressed you?"

"It is not so much what I have seen that has impressed, but what I have not seen," he answered.

Olivia and I exchanged a confused look. What exactly did that mean?

"You want to explain that a little more?" I asked.

"I see water, but there are no rivers or wells or lakes. I see milk, but there are no cows. I see food, but there are no fields or crops or hunters. I see big houses and fancy cars, but no one works. It is like magic that things appear."

"It's far from magic," I said. "The water comes from pipes that are under the ground and bring the water to our houses, same as in Nairobi."

"And the food and milk come from farms that are . . . that are . . . Where *are* the farms?" Olivia asked me.

"Maybe up in the Valley somewhere? At least that's what I think . . . I've never been to them, or even seen them," I admitted. "And people do have jobs."

"I only see Carlos work."

"Other people work, but they work in buildings,

in offices and stores," I explained. I was sure he understood, but I figured he wasn't interested much in what went on in offices. For him, really working probably meant hunting or farming, and nobody did any of that—except for Carlos.

"Now right on Hollywood Boulevard," Olivia said.

I slowed down and almost instantly came to a stop. The traffic was always heavy because of all the tourists who flocked here, causing a traffic jam on both the street and the sidewalks. They were all hoping to see a movie star, but the only things to look at here were the tourist attractions: the Walk of Fame, with all the stars set into the sidewalk; Grauman's Chinese Theatre; and the Kodak Theatre, where the Oscars are given out. They would have had better luck going over to Rodeo, because the rich and famous love to shop.

"Elvis!"

I started and turned around.

Samuel was standing up on the seat, pointing. "Elvis! Elvis!"

"Look out!" Olivia screamed.

I turned back around. The car in front of me had come to a sudden stop! I slammed on the brakes and skidded to a halt just inches from a collision, and Samuel flew forward, landing against the top of the windshield. He windmilled over and then landed on his back on the hood of the car with a thunderous smash!

I froze, terrified, unable to even believe that—

Samuel sat up. He was alive! He turned around and smiled. He was happy and unhurt!

"Elvis!" he screamed again.

He jumped off the car and started running back in the direction we'd come!

"What is he doing?" I screamed. "Where is he going?"

"He saw Elvis," Nebala explained.

"What?"

"Elvis. He saw Elvis . . . there."

"You know Elvis? Samuel knows Elvis?"

"I see him," Olivia said. She was standing on the seat. "I see Samuel, and he's with Elvis."

"How can he be with. . . ?" Then I got it—an Elvis impersonator—one of the celebrity look-alikes who hung out there for the tourists. "He can't just run away. We have to—"

The blaring of a car horn cut me off, and it was joined by a second and then a third. The cars ahead had started moving and I was blocking traffic.

"Olivia, go and get him!" I screamed over the horns, which were growing in number and volume.

Olivia jumped out—and so did Nebala and Koyati. For a split second I almost yelled at them to get back in the car, but really, she might need their help. Besides, they would be all together in one place, and that wasn't bad.

The horns kept blaring and I quickly drove off. I had to find a place to pull over, but where was I going to park on Hollywood Boulevard? There had to be someplace to park here, didn't there? Wait, there was a spot.

I turned the wheel, put my hand on the horn, and bumped up onto the sidewalk as tourists scattered out of the way like a flock of birds. I turned off the car and jumped out, running back along the crowded side-walk. There were mobs of gawking tourists, cameras in hand, wandering or clustered in little knots around the different stars set into the sidewalk, or standing around, posing for pictures with different impersonators.

It was surreal to fly by Superman, and then Elmo, and then a Marilyn Monroe impersonator who looked astonishingly like the real Marilyn, with platinum-blonde hair and a twirly white dress. Maybe if I hadn't been moving so fast I might have seen the flaws.

I caught flashes of red, and then the three Maasai appeared through the crowd. They were all crowded around Elvis.

"Everybody smile!" Olivia sang out, and all four of them—including Koyati—flashed big grins. The strangest thing was seeing Koyati smile—he *never* smiled.

She clicked a picture with her cellphone.

"Let me take one more, just to be sure," she said, and they posed again.

Elvis held his thumbs up in the air. He did look like Elvis—well, the overweight, white-jumpsuit, big-sideburns, Vegas Elvis.

"Great shot!" Olivia said.

She showed me the picture. It was pretty good. All four of the subjects crowded around and looked, nodding their heads in agreement.

"That's a fine picture, young lady," Elvis said. He had the voice down perfectly—a southern gentleman.

He held out his hand toward Olivia. Did he want to shake hands with her?

"Any amount would be appreciated, ma'am," he said.

That's right. They expected people to give them a tip!

"Do you take credit cards?" Olivia asked.

"Do I look like a store?"

His Elvis voice had flattened out and was replaced by a thick New Jersey accent—he sounded sort of like Elvis playing a gangster.

"Sorry, I don't have any cash." Olivia turned to me. "Alexandria, do you have any money?"

"Sure, some . . . maybe."

I opened up my purse and started rummaging around—and my Maasai started to wander off.

"Olivia, stay with them!" I called out. "How much do you charge?" I asked as I pulled out some bills.

"It isn't a specific amount," he said, once again sounding Elvis-like. "Whatever you feel is appropriate."

"Is five dollars appropriate?"

"I would gladly accept that if you felt that was sufficient."

"So you usually get more than that . . . right?"

"Some people, especially when there's more than one person posing with me, very generously provide a twenty-dollar tip."

"Twenty dollars for twenty seconds?" I gasped. "The real Elvis didn't make that much, and he could sing."

"Who says I can't sing?" He grabbed my hand, dropped to one knee, and started crooning to me. *"Love meeee tender . . . love meeee sweeeet . . . never let meeee go!"*

People stopped and stared. Cameras started clicking, and people giggled and pointed.

"That's great," I said, and tried to take back my
hand. He held tight and jerked me forward slightly.
"You can stop now."

"*Yooou have made my life compleeeete . . . aaand I
loooove yooou so!*"

He wasn't stopping—instead he was getting louder.

"*Love meeee tender . . . love meeee true . . . all my dreeee-
aaaams fulfilled!*"

"That's okay, you can stop . . . Please stop!" I begged.

I continued to struggle to get free, but he wrapped
his second hand around my hand, locking it in place.
For a split second I thought about kicking him, but
popping Elvis in front of an adoring crowd didn't
seem right, or smart.

"You can have the twenty dollars," I said, holding
it out to him with my free hand.

He looked up at me and smirked but kept singing
as the crowd cheered him on—that was worth more
to him than the money. He got louder and more
dramatic. I stood there, helpless, at the centre ring in
the Elvis circus. Why couldn't he at least have been
the pre-fried-food, pre-jumpsuit, pre-chubby Elvis?
That man was seriously *hot* in his prime.

He finished the final line with a flourish, and the
crowd went wild, screaming and yelling and whistling
and cheering. He released my hand, and I felt like
cheering too because I was free. He took a bow. I started
to move away when suddenly he grabbed my hand
again, spun me back around, threw his arm around

me, and dipped me back. I could see where this was heading, so before he could kiss me I twisted and ducked under his arm and made my escape, for real this time. Still, the crowd went crazy!

I staggered away through the tourist mob, which parted and applauded as I pushed through. I looked back over my shoulder to see people pressing bills into Elvis's hands.

Up ahead I saw Olivia and the guys. Great, we could all get out of here and— Unbelievable—*they* were now posing for pictures! There were tourists standing around the three of them and having their pictures taken with the Maasai!

"We have to get going before my car gets towed away," I said to Olivia.

"We can't go yet."

"What?"

"I think we need to stay for just a while longer."

"But . . . but why?" I asked.

"Do you think you and Elvis are the only ones making money here?" She held up her hand. It was filled with bills. "So far we've made almost sixty dollars!"

I could hardly believe my eyes, but as I stood there another group of tourists moved into position to have their pictures taken with the Maasai.

"Excuse me," Olivia said to me. "I've got to go and collect some more money. Why don't you move the car someplace and then walk back? Who knows how much we might have earned by then?"

She left me standing there, too stunned to respond, but she was right. I did have to move my car or else—

"Excuse me, ma'am."

I turned. It was Elvis! This was like a nightmare that wouldn't stop. I backed off a step. Why wouldn't he leave me alone? Was this about getting his tip?

"Here, the twenty," I said, offering him the bill that was still in my hand.

"I don't want your money. I want to *give* you money. Here's your cut," he said.

"What?"

"I made over two hundred dollars . . . for one song! Isn't that amazing?" he exclaimed.

"That *is* amazing," I agreed.

"And here's fifty dollars for you." He pressed it into my hands. Once again I was too stunned to speak.

"I hope that's okay. I figure I should keep most of it because I did all the singing and I'm the one in the Elvis suit, but you deserve a cut."

"Umm . . . thanks," I stammered. I looked down at the bills in my hand.

"I was wondering," he said. "Do you think you might want to partner up with me?"

"You want *me* to wear an Elvis suit?" I asked.

He laughed. "No, just show up and let me sing to you, like today."

"I can't do that," I said, shaking my head.

"Don't say no. Just think about it. They loved us!" He beamed. "Here, take my card and think about it. Okay?"

He offered me his card and used that excuse to grab my hand again. Not more singing! I had terrible visions of him bursting into "Blue Suede Shoes."

"Just promise me you'll think about it," he pleaded.

"I promise. I gotta move my car before I get arrested." Or he started singing "Jailhouse Rock."

I ran off toward my car.

"Promise!" he yelled out.

"I promise!" I called back over my shoulder.

CHAPTER NINETEEN

I stood at the front gate, waiting, looking up and down the street. I glanced at my watch. It was almost five. Carlos had told me they'd left just after two o'clock to go on a training run.

If I hadn't been at school when they left I would never have let them go out by themselves. I would have gone along—well, at least driven behind them. Now they were out there by themselves, alone somewhere. They could be lost, or something could have happened to them . . . but then again, this *was* L.A. It wasn't like they were going to run into an elephant or a lion, and even if they did they'd certainly know how to handle it. No, the worst thing they could run into in our neighbourhood was a very large French poodle, and that wouldn't be a problem . . . unless they killed it and brought it home for lunch. Okay, now I was worried again.

"Good afternoon, dear!"

It was my mother, waving her arm above her head in greeting, dressed in her yoga clothing and coming from her Zen garden. I waved back.

I walked out onto the street so I could see farther in both directions. The street was quiet except for the sound of a couple of birds singing in the bushes. Instinctively I looked at my watch again, like somehow that was going to help.

"Are you looking for your friends?" my mother asked.

"Desperately."

"I'm sure there's nothing to worry about. They all have such strong auras."

"Auras?"

"Life force, an energy field that is visible to the eye," she explained.

How was I supposed to respond to that?

"The body has seven chakras, and the soul escapes through trap doors and forms a halo around the body."

"Like an angel?"

She laughed. "In some ways we are *all* angels."

Man, she was getting stranger by the day. Was my mother burning incense in her little Zen garden to cover up what she was smoking?

She took her hands and ran them from my head down both sides of my body, almost but not quite touching me.

"Did you feel that?" she asked.

"You didn't touch me."

"But I did touch your *aura*."

"I didn't know I had one."

"We all have one, and yours is particularly beautiful."

"Thank you." I figured if I *did* have an aura it would have to be beautiful.

"Can you see mine?" she asked.

I looked at her. I couldn't see anything. "Not really."

"It's there. If you meditated with me you would see auras. . . like I can see yours right now, *so* clearly."

I noticed that the sun was behind me and she was sort of looking into it. "It might be the way the bright sun sort of does funny things to your vision. If you were wearing my Gucci sunglasses it would filter it out." I offered her my sunglasses.

She declined the glasses. "In some ways you're right. The quest for material things like those glasses does get in the way of people's auras. Through yoga and meditation, we can rise above the material world."

That would have come across as more legitimate if she hadn't been wearing expensive yoga clothes, standing in front of her mansion in the Hollywood Hills.

"I know. I know what you're thinking," she said. "Who am I to speak about forsaking materialism?"

She was right, and I suddenly felt uncomfortable.

"It's part of my journey. Part of my work." She smiled. "Speaking of work, would you like to see the website?"

"The website? . . . Oh yeah, the website you're making about Nebala and the guys?"

"And their efforts to raise money to build a well."

"I'd *love* to see it," I said. "But not right now . . . I'm a little worried about where they are." I didn't have

time to waste indulging her latest little whim.
Considering that she'd just discovered there even
was an Internet, I didn't hold out much hope for her
web design.

"There's nothing to worry about," she said.
"They're fine."

"I was thinking that I should maybe go out in my
car and have a look for them."

"Let's give them a bit longer. I'm *sure* they're fine."

"I'm just worried that they might be lost. All the
streets here curve around the hills in such a confusing
way. Even people who live here get lost. I could just
go out and drive around—"

"Listen!" she said. She closed her eyes. "Can you
hear?"

Great. Was she *hearing* auras now? All I could hear
were the birds singing in the trees.

"No, I don't—"

"Just close your eyes and listen."

We were still standing in the middle of the road,
and I didn't think that was such a wise thing to do.
Wait . . . I could hear something . . . Was it voices?

"It sounds like singing," my mother said.

"Probably somebody's sound system . . . maybe
their car stereo."

I took her by the hand, and her eyes opened as
I guided her off to the side of the road.

"No," she said, shaking her head, "it's not that."

My mother had closed her eyes again, and I thought
maybe that wasn't such a bad idea. I closed my eyes
too and tried to focus on the sound. It was faint, but

it did seem to be getting louder, closer. It was rhyth-
mic but not really musical. There were voices but no
music. There was no big bass beat behind it like I'd
expect from a car stereo.

"There they are," my mother said.

My eyes popped open, and I looked one way and
then the other . . . and saw them! The three Maasai were
coming toward us, running down the street. As they
ran they were singing. Nebala was calling out a verse and
the other two echoed it back. I'd heard the Maasai
singing similar songs in Kenya. They got closer and closer,
and the singing got stronger and louder and clearer. Not
that I understood the words. They were singing in Maa.

I noticed then that they all were barefoot. Their
new running shoes were tied together and looped
over their necks, bouncing and swaying as they ran.

Nebala raised his hand and they stopped singing
and stopped running, slowing down to a walk.

"Those shoes work better if they're on your feet,"
I said.

"We run better without them," Nebala said.

"You must have run a long way. I was starting to
get a little worried," I said. "I thought you might
get lost."

"Us?" he exclaimed. "Lost? We are—"

"I know, I know. You're Maasai. But this isn't the
Serengeti and you don't know your way around here."

"Is it not the same sun in the sky?" he asked. "Is
this not the same wind that blows?"

"You used the sun and the wind to find your way
back here?" I asked.

"Those and a map."

Samuel produced a glossy-looking map. He handed it to me.

"You had a map of the movie-star homes?" I asked, incredulous.

"We bought it from a man," Nebala said. "Did you know that Rocky lives close to here?"

I didn't know any Rocky.

Samuel started to hum—it was the theme song from the movie *Rocky*!

"You mean Sylvester Stallone?"

"Yes, yes, Rocky! He lives one street over. And there is Tom Cruise and—"

"How do you know all these people?" I asked.

"We are from Kenya, not the planet Mars," he said. "Although even on Mars they must know Elvis is only the second-best singer the world has known."

"Second-best? Who's first?"

"Bob Marley, of course."

"Yes, yes, Bob Marley!" Samuel called out. *"I shot the sherriffff!"* he sang out loudly.

"But I did not shoot the deputy," Koyati chimed in.

I don't know what shocked me more, the Bob Marley or Koyati singing Bob Marley.

"Okay, that's great," I said, trying to silence them.

Nebala joined them in the song, and my mother pulled out her cellphone and began snapping pictures—more shots for her website assignment, I guessed. It was all strange, but it could have been worse. At least there was no Elvis. Still, I wished they would forget about Elvis and Bob Marley and focus on the race . . .

tomorrow was almost here. And this wasn't just a race. This was about winning enough money to build a well so their cows and crops and tribe members could survive . . . winning enough money to buy back their cattle and their manhood. I felt a wave of anxiety swell through my body.

CHAPTER TWENTY

"This is just unbelievable," I said, more to myself than anybody else, as we wandered through the throngs of runners gathering for the race.

"It's wonderful to see so many people taking part in such a wonderful opportunity," my mother said.

"How many people do you think are here?" Olivia asked.

"I heard something on the radio about it being over twenty-five thousand participants," my father answered. "And who knows how many more have come to watch? I heard there might be somewhere between a hundred and two hundred thousand spectators."

Olivia and both of my parents had come down to offer their support. It was great to have them all here. It was strange about my parents. Not that long ago, putting them in the same place at the same time would have been the only ingredients necessary to cook up a big fight.

"You didn't all need to come down," I offered.

"I wouldn't have missed this for the world," Olivia said.

"And I just wanted to make sure that there were no, shall we say, complications," my father added.

"They're official."

All three had their tracking chips, and their entry numbers were pinned to their chests. They all were also wearing their original shoes, the tire-tread sandals. They found that they just couldn't run with those fancy shoes on their feet. Dakota and his shoe sponsor wouldn't be happy if those three found themselves on the victory podium wearing their sandals. The sponsor's high-tech, space-age-material, super-expensive, super-advertised sports footwear was basically the Prada of running shoes.

An announcement came over the P.A. system: "Runners, please report to your assigned sections."

"What does that mean?" I asked.

Everybody shrugged. Nobody knew.

"Let's ask him," Olivia said, pointing to a man. "He looks official."

With his orange vest, and carrying a big walkie-talkie that looked like an old-school cellphone, he did have that official quality.

"Excuse me," my father said to him. "Where do our runners go?"

"Each runner reports to his or her starting-grid position," the man replied.

"And that means?" my father questioned.

"We can't have everybody start at the same time and same place or there'd be a stampede, so there are different grid spots, with the fastest runners starting from the front positions and those with slower qualifying times starting farther back."

Suddenly I had a very bad feeling.

"And how do we know where they start?" my father said, pointing to the Maasai.

"By the entry number that they were assigned," he said. "Let me have a look at your numbers and I can tell you their grid spot."

I already knew where they were going to be. "What's the last grid spot?" I asked.

"Ten . . . and that's where you three are going to be starting. Grid ten."

"But that means there are over twenty thousand runners who will be in front of them," I said.

"Closer to twenty-*two* thousand runners," the official said.

"What is the name of that *gentleman* whom I was dealing with, the director of this race?" my father asked.

"Dakota Rivers," I said.

"Dakota Rivers," my father repeated slowly. "When I find him, he's going to severely regret ever crossing me. I'm going to find him right now and have him change their starting place or—"

"The race is going to start in less than five minutes," the official said. "If they don't get to their grid positions before race time they'll be disqualified."

"With all these people out here it might be very hard for anybody to tell just where exactly they started from," my father said.

I knew his mind was already spinning, looking for a way around this.

"No, it wouldn't," the official said.

"You're going to tell?" my father asked.

"The *chip* is going to tell."

We all exchanged confused looks.

"The chip contains a global positioning system, so the computer link knows exactly where they are at all times during the race . . . including the start of the race. If they're not in their grid they *will* be disqualified." He looked at his watch. "And they have less than three minutes to get there. They'd *really* better hurry. In fact, come with me and I'll lead you there just to make sure. Come."

He started off through the crowd, and we all rushed after him—a funny little parade of me, Olivia, the three Maasai, and both my parents moving through a sea of runners. They were all warming up—stretching and bending and doing little fast steps. Some seemed to be lost in thought, while others were laughing and talking and practically vibrating, waiting with excitement for the start.

"Make way!" the official called out. "Let us through!"

The people parted and made a path for us.

"Excuse me," I said to him. "I know this is the first year for this marathon, but do you know if anybody has ever started that far back in any marathon and won?"

"I don't know the results of all marathons," he said.

"But the ones you know of?"

"None that I know of . . . but there's always a first time, I guess."

We continued to weave through the crowd. We were the only people who weren't in spandex and sneakers—Olivia, my mother, and I wore designer clothes; my father was dressed in a suit; and the three Maasai were in their brilliant red clothing. Runners turned to watch us pass. We were quite a sight.

"Here we are," the official said. "Tenth grid spot."

"Thanks for all your help," I said.

"I'm here for the runners. I wish you three the best. Good luck, gentlemen."

He shook hands with them and walked away, disappearing into the crowd.

"One minute to start!" came another P.A. announcement.

"We'd better get out of here before they start or we'll be stampeded," Olivia said.

"We'll be okay."

"Don't you remember that scene in *Lion King*?" she asked. "That's how they got Simba's dad."

"I don't see any wildebeest, so I think we're okay," I said. "Nebala, you know we're going to keep moving along the route. Like we discussed, you'll see us every five miles, and we'll try to give you information about how many people are still in front of you."

He nodded.

"Remember, you have to keep up a five-minute-mile pace to win. There are big clocks at every mile, so you'll be able to know your pace."

"We do not need clocks. We will run as fast as we can."

"You have to pace yourself."

"We have to run until there are no more runners in front. That is our pace."

"Are you sure you remember the route . . . where to run?"

"We will follow other runners until just before the end. And then we will pass them."

"You'll have to run *very* fast to win."

"We will win," he said. "We *have* to win."

"I know."

"Thirty seconds!" the P.A. called out.

"Come on, quickly, before we get trampled to death," Olivia pleaded.

"We'd better get going now," my mother said, "or we won't be able to get to the first spot along the route before they get there."

Now that was something that did make sense.

I wanted to give them one final word of encouragement, say something smart or inspirational. Instead I reached up and gave Nebala a hug, then Samuel, and finally Koyati.

We started working our way to the very back of the crowd. We didn't have to move very far. We were almost at the very, very back of the pack.

"Runners, take your mark!" the P.A. sounded.

I looked back through the mass of runners. Thanks to their bright-red clothing, the three Maasai were easily visible, just ten or fifteen yards ahead of us. Looking beyond them I saw a sea of runners stretching to the horizon. Wherever the first runners were, I couldn't see them. All I did know was that there were over twenty thousand runners standing between Nebala and the finish line.

A gun sounded and I jumped slightly as the entire throng of people came to life and started moving. I watched as the crowd surged forward, en masse, like one big, living organism instead of thousands of individuals.

"Do you think they can win?" my mother asked.

"It's going to be awfully difficult," my father answered.

"No," I said, shaking my head. "They'll win."

"How can you be so certain?" Olivia asked.

"I just am. We'd better get to the car."

CHAPTER TWENTY-ONE

"You girls should get out right here," my father said as he pulled the car to the curb. "Just walk toward the crowd."

"Thanks," I said as Olivia and I climbed out.

"I'll be right here waiting to drive you to the next checkpoint."

"I'm coming too!" my mother said, and she jumped out of the car to join us.

"You'd better run. It's been over twenty minutes since the race started," my father called out after us.

I closed the door, and the three of us ran toward the crowd lining the road up ahead. There was a wall of people at least five or six rows deep. Through the heads and shoulders of the spectators I could make out little glimpses of runners passing by. That didn't make sense; nobody should have been this far this fast, but some runners had already come and gone.

From where we stood I couldn't tell how many runners had passed. Worse still, I wouldn't be able to see or help our guys. We had to get to the front, and there was only one way to do that. When in doubt, just act like you own the place.

"Excuse us," I said to the person directly in front of me. "We have to get through."

A few people turned around, but nobody moved. A couple just gave us dirty looks.

"Please let us by," I commanded, trying for a mix of polite, official, and regal—people would always let royalty through, and I *was*, in fact, a California princess. Nobody moved. Apparently either they were disputing my sovereignty, or everybody in Beverly Hills felt like they were royalty, too.

"This is no good; we have to get through," I said to my mother and Olivia.

"Maybe I can help," my mother said.

"I'm not quite sure how yoga could help this situation," I said sarcastically.

"Yoga helps in almost *all* situations. If these people were less stressed and more centred they wouldn't object to us passing. But we don't have time for that right now. Follow me."

Reluctantly I followed behind as she walked along the back of the crowd. I didn't have time for this. I needed to somehow break through. Maybe if I yelled or—

"Press!" my mother yelled. "Let us through. We're with Channel Seven News!"

People in the crowd turned around. She held up her camera like it was proof of some sort.

There was no way that this was going to— Wow, two people in the back shifted to the side to create an opening!

"Thank you!" my mother said.

She moved forward and we followed behind as row after row the crowd shifted and separated until we got to the front. We were blocked by a thin blue rope that separated the runners and the watchers. My mother ducked underneath and then held the rope up to allow me and Olivia to follow.

"That was impressive, Mrs. H.," Olivia said.

"Thank you, dear. Now, you girls look for the boys. I want to get some more pictures."

We walked a few paces away from the rope and onto the course. The runners were basically moving down the middle of the boulevard. The blob of runners that had started the race had thinned out to a long line no more than a dozen or so runners wide, stretching out of sight in both directions. There were a lot of runners out there, and lots of runners who had already gone by.

"I don't see them," Olivia said.

"Me neither."

"Do you think it's possible that they've already passed this spot?"

I looked up at the clock marking Mile Five. Big glowing numbers ticked out the time that had passed—twenty-three minutes and thirty-seven . . . thirty-eight . . . thirty-nine seconds.

"It would be great if they had gone this far this fast, but I don't think so. Let's just keep watching for them."

I looked back through the runners. There were so many of them, and with each second more people passed by—runners who were in front of them, more runners they had to pass if they were going to win. With each second it seemed less possible that they could catch everybody. Could they really do it?

"How many people do you think have already gone past this spot?" Olivia asked.

I shook my head. "There's no way to—"

"Excuse me, ladies, you have to get back behind the rope."

I looked over. It was another one of the race officials—the same orange vest, same big walkie-talkie as the other guy.

I wasn't stepping back anywhere. "Could you tell me how many runners have passed by already?"

"Close to two thousand runners."

"Two thousand runners! Are you sure?" I asked.

"That's just an educated guess, but a good one. I've been here watching throughout the entire race."

"How long ago did the first runners pass by?" I asked.

"Almost two minutes ago. They did a fast first five—four-thirty splits."

"What does that mean?" Olivia asked.

"They ran the first five miles with an average time of four minutes and thirty seconds."

I gasped. There was no way our Maasai could run that fast, was there? And I'd told them that they only had to run five-minute miles. What if they lost because they'd listened to me?

"But . . . but . . . that's impossible," I stammered. I'd read all about marathons, and he had to be wrong. "Nobody can run a whole marathon at that pace."

"They won't keep up that pace," he agreed. "They always start fast to get ahead of the pack. If you get caught among the slower participants you have no chance of catching the front runners."

I wanted to ask him what chance you had if you started so far back that you had to run fast even to catch the slow runners, but I was afraid I knew the answer. They could be way back, trapped, not able to weave through the pack.

There was a toot of a horn, and we all looked up to see a motorcycle coming along the side of the road toward us. We flattened against the rope and the crowd as it passed. There was a passenger, riding backwards, holding a big camera and filming the racers.

"I'm afraid you ladies really need to get back. I don't want you to be run over by one of the race vehicles," he said as he started to shoo us back.

"We won't get hit, and we can't go back," I said firmly. "They won't see us if we're lost in the crowd."

"It's nice that you want to support your friends, but if everybody did that the whole race would be nothing but chaos."

"That's why it's great that not everybody *is* doing it. Couldn't we just stay for another minute? They'll be here soon, promise."

He looked as though he was thinking it through.

"Please?" I said. I smiled and tilted my head to one side, trying my best to flirt with him. "You could stay right here with us to make sure we're okay . . . pleeease?"

He let out a big sigh. "Maybe for a minute or two. Your friends must be good runners. Are you sure they haven't passed?"

"I doubt it!" Olivia said. "Not judging from how far back they started in the pack."

That was stupid. Why had she told him that? Why had she told him anything?

"How far back were they?" he asked. He sounded concerned.

"They were almost in the very last row," I confessed. "The official at the start said something about them being in the tenth grid."

"Then you'd better step back under the rope right now because there's no way that anybody starting from that far back could ever get here nearly this soon."

"They're really good runners!" I pleaded. "They just got placed back there because they didn't have qualifying times."

"You mean they've never even run a marathon before?" he asked, sounding like he couldn't believe his ears.

"They've never run a timed marathon, but they can run five-minute miles, so they should be here almost right now," I said. "Just look at the clock."

The big clock at the five-mile marker was just fifteen seconds short of twenty-five minutes.

"You don't understand," he said. "Even if they can run five-minute miles there's no way they could move that quickly from the back of the pack. There are hundreds—no, thousands, *tens* of thousands—of runners ahead of them, getting in their way, blocking their path, slowing them down. Now please, ladies, just step behind—"

His words were cut short by a roar from the crowd. What were they all so excited about?

"There they are!" the official said.

"There *who* are?" I asked.

He laughed. "This is so strange you won't believe it . . . but I heard they were in the race."

"Heard what? Who's in the race?"

"Apparently there are three Maasai warriors running the marathon! They're in traditional costumes and wearing shoes that are made out of old car tires! Can you believe that?"

I looked onto the course. There they were!

"Yeah, I think I can believe it," I said. I took a couple of steps toward the runners. "Nebala!" I yelled out.

"Wait! You can't run onto the course!" the official screamed.

I ignored him and ran out onto the road, waving my arms in the air to make sure they could see me.

All three of them changed course and angled toward me. They were almost on top of me now. Their mouths were wide open, their faces twisted in anguish, sweat running down their faces. Suddenly my mother was right at my side and she was snapping pictures like crazy.

"There are still over two thousand runners in front of you!" I yelled to Nebala. "You have to run the next five miles even faster! Faster!"

They kept running without acknowledging what I had said. Did they hear me? Did they understand?

"You have to run faster! Do you understand?"

"Faster," Nebala huffed. "Yes . . . yes . . . faster . . . faster."

They ran right by me without missing a stride, and I spun around to watch them run. My mother continued to snap pictures as they passed.

There was a hand on my arm. It was the official. "You know the Maasai?" he questioned.

"I'm sort of their trainer."

"Wow," he gasped. He looked genuinely impressed. "And is it true? Are they really Maasai from Kenya?"

"Yes, from the Maasai Mara in Kenya."

"And they came here to try to raise money for a well."

"Yes, that's why they're— Wait . . . how do *you* know that?" I questioned.

"It was on the website."

"Website? They were mentioned on the race website?"

"Not the Beverly Hills Marathon website. It was the Maasai website. It was all about the three of them—Nebala and Samuel and . . . I can't remember the name of the third runner."

"His name is Koyati," my mother said.

"Yes, Koyati."

"And it sounds like you enjoyed the website," she said. "I'm the webmaster."

"You did an amazing job!" he exclaimed.

"Thank you," she said, beaming. "That was the first website I've ever constructed."

"That's even more amazing! You really have a talent!"

"Again, thank you so much."

"How did you find out about the website?" I asked him.

"I googled the official site and the Maasai marathon site came up right below it, so I just looked. A lot of people have looked."

"There have been quite a lot of hits," my mother said. "It surprised me how it just sort of took off."

"It's a great story and a great website, so it's no surprise that people are clicking on it," the official said. "I think your friends' involvement has captured a lot of people's attention. Everybody along the whole route is so excited about them being in the race!" he exclaimed.

"I don't know about *everybody*." That certainly didn't include the race director.

"No," he said, shaking his head. "Everybody. They're the talk of the race. Didn't you hear the cheer as they went by? The crowd is loving them!"

"Yeah, I guess they are. Speaking of which, we have to move along. We've got to get to the ten-mile mark before they do."

We started to walk toward the rope, keeping an eye open for random motorcycles and runners.

"Hold on!" the official called out as he caught up to us. "I have an idea. Just wait by the rope."

"We don't have time to wait. We have to get to the car, find a route to the ten-mile mark, and then get through the crowd again, so—"

"Just wait a minute. Maybe I can help."

Before I could even ask him how, he turned away and started walking down the rope. He pulled out his big walkie-talkie and was calling out for somebody on the other end.

"What do you think he's doing?" Olivia asked.

"I'm not sure, but I'm a little bit nervous. Maybe we should just slip under the rope and get back to the car." His back was to us and he was still talking on the walkie-talkie. "He won't even notice we're gone."

"No," my mother said. "We should wait. I have a good feeling about this."

"Does he have a good aura?" I asked.

"Yes, he does, but he has an even better attitude. Let's wait."

"I don't know. If we don't leave soon . . . "

"Let's give him two minutes to do the right thing. If it doesn't work we'll just have your father drive faster. You know how much he'd love an excuse to drive that sports car really, really fast."

"I guess we're okay for a minute or so," I agreed.

I looked up. The official had stepped out from the rope and was waving his arms in the air like he was trying to bring in an airplane. There were more and more runners, and then I saw a little vehicle—it was a golf cart. It was streaming along the side of the roadway. As it approached I could hear the high-pitched whine getting louder and louder. Boy, was that guy ever travelling fast.

The official stepped out, putting himself in the path of the cart to block it. That was probably smart. Somebody needed to stop that guy before he ran over one of the runners. The golf cart came to a squealing stop right in front of us.

The official turned to us and smiled. "Your chariot awaits," he said as he bowed from the waist.

"A golf cart? But we have a ride. My father is waiting for us just over there." I gestured in the direction of our car—a really, really nice, expensive car.

"The big difference is that the car is over *there*. The cart is right *here*."

"Maybe the cart could take us to our car," I suggested, trying to not sound mean or ungrateful.

"You don't understand. You don't need your car. The driver will take you right along the course. You can follow your runners every step of the way. You can tell them their times," he said to me. "And you can take more pictures for the website," he said to my mother.

I was speechless. This was amazing.

"But you're free to go and take the car, if that's what you want. It's up to you, but the cart is yours to use." He paused. "Well?"

I threw my arms around him and gave him a big hug. I still couldn't find any words, but I could give him an answer.

CHAPTER TWENTY-TWO

The driver tooted his little horn, and a few of the people got out of his way—some didn't.

"Hang on!" he called out.

I grabbed the sidebar and held on as he swerved to the side to avoid the remaining spectators. We weren't the only people who had wandered onto the wrong side of the rope.

"Do you see them?" Olivia asked.

"Not yet."

I was riding beside the driver. Olivia and my mother were sitting on the back of the cart, facing backwards. My mother was furiously snapping pictures.

We'd called my father to tell him what we were doing. He was going to meet us at the finish line—he was really hoping to find Dakota there, waiting. I would have liked to have been there myself to hear exactly what my father was going to say, but I was sure he'd tell me all about it afterward. I almost pitied Dakota. Okay, not really. He was going to get what he deserved.

"Do you think we could have passed them?" Olivia suggested.

"No chance. I would have had to miss them coming, and you and Mom would have had to miss them going."

"They'd be pretty hard to miss," the driver said. "I'm sure they're still up ahead. Do you know their pace?"

"They did the first five in twenty-five minutes," I answered.

"There's the seven-mile marker just up ahead," he said.

I saw the big clock. It read out thirty-six minutes and twenty-five seconds. If they had kept up the five-minute-mile pace, then they would be just a few hundred yards ahead.

"Are they really running with tire-tread sandals?" the driver asked.

"Yeah. How did you know that's what they're wearing?"

"The website. It's got all kinds of graphics and information!"

"I heard."

I wish I'd actually looked at it one of those times my mother had asked me to. That would be the first thing I'd do as soon as I got home.

"Can you get on your walkie-talkie and ask where they are?"

"It's supposed to be used only for official race business."

I'd been listening to the constant static-filled conversation that was coming out of it, and a whole lot of it didn't sound business-related.

"This is race business, if you think about it," I suggested. "Couldn't you just go on for a second and ask?"

"I could, but I don't think it'll be necessary. I think they're just up ahead. In fact, I'm sure. Listen."

I wasn't sure what he expected me to hear. Between the voices over the walkie-talkie, the whining of the engine of the golf cart, and the cheering of the crowd . . . The crowd—why was the crowd cheering so loudly?

"There they are!" the driver yelled.

Instantly I saw them. Those red costumes were just so bright and so different from the sea of spandex that surrounded them that they were incredibly easy to pick out.

As we closed in I could see—and hear—how the crowd reacted to them. It was like a gigantic wave sweeping down both sides of the road as the spectators saw them and burst into applause and cheers.

"We need to get closer," I said.

"I'm driving as fast as I can."

"But can't you swing out into the middle of the boulevard?"

"That I can't do. I have to stay at the side of the course."

We were almost parallel with them, but too far

away to tell them much. They hadn't even noticed us, and my voice would have just been lost in the swelling sound of the cheers.

"Get us far enough in front of them and then stop. I'll run out to see them," I suggested.

"That I *can* do."

He pushed down the pedal, and I was pressed back into the seat with the acceleration. That little golf cart could really move. Now we'd just have to get far enough ahead.

"Do you know where the front runners are?" I asked.

"Not exactly sure, but my best guess, judging from the time—it's about forty minutes since the start—they'd be just past the eight-mile mark."

"Then they're not that far ahead!" I exclaimed. That was good news—no, it was great news! But our driver kind of squashed that good feeling.

"One mile is a big distance. Races are won and lost by seconds and yards, not minutes and miles."

"But at least they're in shouting distance . . . more or less."

"That's a lot more than it is less."

Olivia leaned over the seat. "So what place would they be in?"

"Place?" he asked.

"You know, how many runners are still in front of our Maasai?"

"Now that would be very hard to tell, but again, my best guess, maybe three or four."

"Three or four hundred?"

He laughed. "Three or four *thousand*."

"That's really not that bad," I said. I was trying to sound optimistic.

"That's not so good, either," Olivia countered.

"It is, if you think about it. Let's take the worst case and say there are four thousand runners in front of them. That means that they've already passed seventeen thousand."

"Twenty-five minus four equals twenty-one. The math makes sense, but it still doesn't sound good," Olivia said.

"Okay, try this, then. They have already passed 84 percent of all the runners in the race."

"And 16 percent are still ahead of them," Olivia said. "Even I can do simple math."

"Here's the good part. With every mile they ran they passed 12 percent of the participants. That's over three thousand runners every mile. So that means that at their present speed, they should be at the front in less than two miles. So by the time they hit the ten-mile mark they'll—"

"Still be way behind at least a thousand runners," the driver said, cutting me off.

"No, that's not right. I've done the math and I know my numbers are right," I protested.

"She's always right with numbers," Olivia said to the driver. "If Gucci made a calculator it would look like Alexandria."

That was quite the compliment!

"I'm sure your friend is very good with numbers, but she's wrong here."

"I am not wrong!" I protested indignantly. "I'll try to explain it to you. Approximately every quarter of the mile is one percent of the race," I said.

"Every .26 of a mile," the driver said.

"I said *approximately* every quarter of a mile. So every .26 of a mile is one percent of the entire race. And assuming they have passed twenty-two thousand people, which is 84 percent of the race, and they have done that in seven miles, which is 26.93 percent of the total distance, then—"

"Did you just do that in your head?" he asked.

"Yes."

"You should see her at a shoe sale. She can calculate the sale price of a pair of Prada pumps faster than the cash register," Olivia said. "Alexandria is never wrong about math."

"I'm not arguing with her math. Her numbers are correct."

"How do you know that she's right?" Olivia asked. "I don't see *you* using any calculator."

"I don't need a calculator. I teach differential equations in the engineering department at UCLA. Math is my life."

"I'm confused," I said. "If you know my calculations are correct, then why do you think my result is wrong?"

"It's not your math that I'm contesting. It's your understanding," the driver said. "You're assuming constant variables that are, in fact, *not* constant."

"What?"

"Let me explain. You're assuming that all twenty-five thousand race participants are equal, but they're not.

Your runners have thus far passed the twenty-two thousand *slowest* runners. They are going to find it increasingly difficult to pass each participant who is in front of them. And they will need increasingly larger quantities of time and distance to pass every successive participant. Does that make sense?"

"Not at all," Olivia said. "Alexandria?"

"I'm afraid it does," I reluctantly admitted.

"And that doesn't even take into account that you are not certain if they can maintain this pace for the entire length of the race," he said. "They have already expended a great deal of energy to gain ground on the front runners, who, realistically, have run almost two hundred yards less than the Maasai because of the stagger between the first and tenth grids. So, logically, mathematically, for them to actually win this race the odds are staggeringly against—"

"But this *isn't* just about the numbers," I snapped. "You don't know about the Maasai, or you'd never bet against them."

"I'm sorry, I wasn't betting against them. I'd love to see them win. It's just that logically—"

"Logic is the same as numbers. What they're doing isn't about the head; it's about the heart."

"I hope you're right. I'm going to stop just up ahead at the ten-mile marker."

I looked up. I'd been so busy arguing that I hadn't been paying attention to the road or the runners. I saw the clock. It was coming up to fifty minutes. And looking down the road, beyond the clock, I realized that I couldn't see any runners ahead of us.

"Has anybody passed this marker yet?" I asked.

"Not likely," the driver said. "Do you see those runners to our side?"

I looked over. "Yeah." There were three men running one after the other with only feet between them.

"The man in the lead won the gold medal in the last Olympics."

"Wow."

"The two men behind him, they're the current and former world record holders. Between the three of them they hold the records for the fastest times in over eight marathons, including Boston and New York."

"Double wow."

They were running fast and apparently effortlessly. I looked back, hoping to miraculously see Nebala and the boys closing ground. There was a clump of runners, maybe fifty or sixty men, two hundred yards back, but no Maasai.

"Do you think your runners can catch these guys?" the driver asked.

I had an answer. I just didn't want to say it. Or even admit it to myself.

CHAPTER TWENTY-THREE

Our driver pulled the golf cart off to the very side of the boulevard, tight to the rope and directly under the big, blinking, ticking clock. I jumped off before he'd completely come to a stop and stumbled forward, almost losing my footing. Perhaps heels weren't the wisest footwear for a marathon, even if I was only a spectator . . . but they were such *nice* heels.

The first three runners were almost upon us. Free of all the other runners, they were moving amazingly fast. If I hadn't seen it with my own eyes I wouldn't have believed it.

"You can tell by the way they move," the driver said. "They don't run as much as *glide*."

I watched as they got closer. He was right. "Running" was hardly the right word to describe their motion. It seemed so effortless. They certainly

didn't look as though they'd just covered ten miles—
and done it in way less than fifty minutes. That was
almost unbelievable.

A round of applause erupted as they passed along
the route. It was loud, but not as loud as the cheers
that had been following my Maasai.

"Mom, I need you to take a picture of the clock
when the first three runners pass by."

"If you want, but I don't really know if it's such a
wonderful shot."

"I want you to take the picture so we can snap
another picture when Nebala passes by. That way we'll
know, to the second, how far they're behind."

"That's a great idea," Olivia said. "Is there anything
I can do?"

"Yes. I need you to count the runners."

"All of them?" she gasped.

"All of them until Nebala and Samuel and Koyati
pass by. I need to know exactly how many runners are
in front of them."

"I don't know if I can count them all . . . What if I
miss a few?"

"That's okay. Just sort of get a rough count. Do the
best you can."

The front runners got closer, and the people
around us started to clap and cheer them on. I felt like
booing, or maybe sticking a foot way, way out and
trying to trip them. That wouldn't have been very
sporting, and it wouldn't have worked, and it also
would have potentially ruined a simply spectacular
pair of Prada pumps.

"Take the picture of the clock now," I said to my mother.

It read 46:45. They were doing each mile at just under a four-minute, forty-second pace. That was incredible . . . incredibly awful. Even if the Maasai had picked up their pace—by almost thirty seconds a mile—they'd still have fallen even *farther* behind the leaders.

"Are you counting, Olivia?"

"So far the magic number is three, but that's going to change soon."

Down the road, closing fast, was the pack of runners. I tried to do a quick count. There might have been thirty, maybe forty-five. They were all bunched in together so closely that they looked like one large organism with multiple heads bobbing and legs pumping, all wrapped within a bizarrely coloured spandex skin.

They ran by to renewed cheering from the crowd lining the route. I looked up at the clock: 47:20.

"I think that was about fifty," Olivia said.

I wasn't going to argue. That was close enough.

"Do any of those guys have a chance to win?" I asked our driver.

"A number of runners—including a few I know are in that pack—are sprint specialists. If they can get to within thirty or forty seconds of the front runners during the last mile or so they can kick into a much faster gear and overcome the leaders."

It was good to know that he felt somebody could still beat the three front runners. Although as we stood there a steady stream of other runners raced past us, and none of them were our Maasai.

"You still counting?"

"Still trying . . . not easy . . . ninety-four . . . ninety-five, six, and seven."

There was a steady line of runners racing down the road. It wasn't a stream, but it was more than a trickle. And none of them were Maasai.

I climbed up onto the side of the golf cart so I could get more height and see farther back down the boulevard. I still didn't see them. With each second, more runners were passing by.

I started thinking about what they were trying to do. I knew how hard it was to run a marathon. I knew how many thousands of runners—good runners . . . no, *great* runners . . . no, no, world *champion* runners—were in this race, but I'd always just thought that my guys were going to cross the finish line first. After all, as they liked to point out, they were Maasai. Now, standing here, I wasn't sure. Not that I was counting them out, but really, could they pass all these runners and win?

Then again, they didn't have to win the marathon; they just had to win enough money to pay for their well. And of course the airfare back. And some cows to make up for the ones they'd sold to get here. Even with all that, it wasn't that much money.

"Excuse me," I asked the driver. "I know how much money the first few racers get, but do lots of people get prize money?"

"I think there's money for the first two dozen places."

"So even runner number twenty-four takes home money?" This was wonderful news.

"I think around ten thousand."

"That's pretty good money," I said.

I did a little mental calculation. Three airplane tickets at $2,800 per ticket would be $8,400—that would leave $1,600, which would be enough to buy almost twenty cows. That wouldn't be enough to replace their herds, but it would be a start ... although there would be no money to drill a well. Still, they could go home. Maybe come back another year and try.

Or maybe they could finish twenty-second, twenty-third, and twenty-fourth, and then they would have enough money. All they had to do was finish behind twenty-one other runners. Let the Olympic gold medallist, the two world record holders, some sprint specialists, and a few other assorted runners beat them, and they could still drill the well and return home as champions.

"I think I see them," my mother said.

I craned my neck to look as far as I could. The distance was a little blurry. I was starting to think I might need glasses. I didn't want to admit that, even to myself. I knew there were wonderful designer frames available, and lots of the beautiful people wore them, but glasses were never going to be in— Oh, there they were!

They were running single file. Nebala was leading, then came Koyati, and Samuel was just a step behind.

"Olivia, how many runners have passed?" I asked.

"Around seven hundred and fifty."

"Are you sure?" I snapped.

"I'm not sure of anything. It could be seven hundred

or it could be eight hundred and fifty. That's just my best guess."

"Sorry."

Next I looked at the clock: 49:31 and counting.

I jumped off the cart and ran—as fast as my little heeled feet would carry me—until I was standing in the boulevard, with other runners brushing by me. The Maasai were getting closer and closer and closer. Nebala looked up, saw me, and waved and smiled. That was so good. After ten miles he was still smiling.

The ripple of applause built as they came closer. It was loud—much louder than it had been even for the *leaders*.

"You're doing great!" I yelled out. "You've already passed over twenty-four thousand runners!"

I thought it was better to tell them how many they'd passed rather than how many more they still had to get in front of. There was plenty of time for that, and maybe by the fifteen-mile mark there would be a lot fewer people in front.

They'd be here and then past me in a few seconds, and I needed to say more. I'd have to run along with them. I could do that for a couple of dozen yards . . . if I wasn't wearing heels.

They were practically on top of me. I kicked off my heels and ran in my bare feet.

"How are you doing?" I asked as I started to run beside Nebala.

"We are doing."

"Are you feeling okay . . . Are you doing okay?"

"Okay."

"Good. Good. You're doing good . . . but you have to run faster!" I said.

"Faster?" Nebala spun his head to face me.

"Yes, faster. You have to run faster."

I was struggling to keep up with them. How could anybody possibly run so fast for so long?

"Can you run faster?" I asked.

"We are Maasai."

Nebala barked out a word in Swahili and then he picked up the pace, and as Koyati and Samuel matched his pace I started to fade. I couldn't keep up. I didn't need to keep up.

"Keep running!" I yelled.

I started to slow down and was bumped suddenly from behind.

"Sorry!" a man yelled as he brushed by me.

I scrambled over to the side, nearly colliding with another runner en route as I managed to get out of the flow of the runners. Safely over by the rope I doubled over and tried to catch my breath. And I'd run with them for only thirty seconds!

The golf cart came whizzing up, with my mother and Olivia looking over the back seat toward me. The driver came to a stop right beside me.

"Jump in!" the driver said.

"I can't. I have to go back to get my shoes." That was three hundred dollars' worth of Italian leather lying there in the middle of the street.

"I retrieved them," Olivia said, holding them up.

I climbed in. "Thanks, that was so— What happened to my Pradas?" I gasped as I took them. The leather was all scuffed up and there was a little rip on the side of one of them.

"I think they were stepped on."

"By an elephant?"

"By a number of runners who didn't see them on the road," the driver said. "We're just lucky that nothing serious happened."

"Nothing?" I asked. "Look at these shoes! They're practically *ruined*!"

"But nobody tripped or fell down or was injured," the driver said. "That would have been serious."

Okay, I understood what he meant.

"I should have got them sooner," Olivia apologized.

"It's not your fault. Thanks for getting them as soon as you did. Let's get going."

The driver put the cart into gear, and we jumped forward as if the little vehicle had been stung by a bee. I slipped my shoes back on.

"I got some great shots as they passed," my mother said. "They'll look fantastic on the website."

"Have you thought about doing that for a living?" the driver asked.

"Photography?"

"No, website design."

Now I was feeling even guiltier about not having looked at it.

"Right now, I just hope that this website's story has a happy ending," my mother said.

"You mean with them winning the marathon?" the driver asked.

"That would be—"

"Do you think they could do that?" I asked, cutting off my mother.

"I think they've done very, very well . . . *so far*. I mean, to start in the last grid and get this far, at this pace, is in itself a major victory."

"But you still don't think they can win, do you?"

"If you look at things objectively they're still a tremendous long shot. They've never even run a marathon before, so we don't know if they can run the distance."

"Oh, they can run that far, believe me."

"But can they run that far at the pace they set for the first ten miles?" he asked. "That's the question."

It was. I only wished I had an answer.

CHAPTER TWENTY-FOUR

The second group of runners—a total of about twenty-five—passed by. I looked at the clock: 1:15:30. These runners were now over a minute and fifteen seconds behind the three in front. They had lost thirty-three seconds in their race to catch the leaders. That didn't matter much. What really mattered was how far back *our* guys were. I didn't see them yet. In fact, I didn't really see that many runners. There was a thin, straggly line of runners spread out into the distance.

"You're counting, right, Olivia?"

"I'm counting. Do you see them?"

"Not yet."

"Have they fallen farther behind?"

"Don't know. Don't see them."

"But weren't they only a couple of minutes behind at the ten-mile mark?" she asked.

"Two minutes and forty-six seconds behind the leaders, and two minutes and eleven seconds behind the second group."

"How do all those numbers stick in your head?"

"They just do."

There was a honk and I started, jumping out of the way, but there was no cart. The horn sounded again and I spun around. A little golf cart was coming toward us from the other direction—going against the flow of the runners and all the other race vehicles. He laid on the horn again. Why was he honking? He wasn't even close to us.

Then I recognized the driver. It was Dakota Rivers! His cart squealed to a stop right beside me, and Dakota jumped out. His being here could mean nothing good. Was he going to kick us off the course, or try to disqualify our runners? I wasn't going to let him get started. The best defence, I knew, is often an offence.

"You have some nerve showing up!" I exclaimed.

He looked surprised by my response. That was good.

"My father is looking for you at the finish line. Is that why you're out here, so you can hide from him?"

"I'm not hiding from anybody. Actually, I came out looking for you."

"Me?"

"Well, you and those Maasai."

"You'd better not try to interfere with them in any way . . . or *else*. As it is, there's hardly any hope that my father isn't going to sue you. The nerve of you to put them in the last grid position!"

"Where else would I put runners with no qualifying times?"

"So why are you here?"

"I just wanted to see how our Maasai runners are doing."

"*Our* runners? Don't you mean *my* runners?"

"Everybody in this race is one of our runners."

"Like you even wanted them in your race to begin with!" I huffed.

"I certainly *am* pleased that they're in the race."

I gave him a look of total disbelief.

"I'm serious," he said. "The press is just eating this up. They are becoming *quite* the story."

"A story you didn't want told, because you didn't think it had enough class for your marathon!" I snapped.

"I'm so sorry if you got that impression. I certainly never met to imply that."

"Imply?" I scoffed. "Those were your *exact* words."

"Words can be so ... so ... Look, here they come!"

I spun around. There they were!

"Olivia!" I called out. "How many people?"

"Four hundred and fifty-seven just passed ... and they will be the—let me count—the sixty-ninth, seventieth, and four hundred and seventy-first runners."

"That's great." I looked up at the clock: 1:16:29. I did a quick estimate and mental calculation. If they got here within ten seconds they would have gained almost one minute and ten seconds on the second group. That was amazing, to close the gap that fast in five miles!

What wasn't so amazing was that they really hadn't gained much on the three front runners. They were still more than two minutes behind. At this rate there was no way that they were going to catch them. But of course, they didn't have to catch them to take home prize money. I had to remind myself that they just had to get into the top twenty to collect enough money for what they needed.

I kicked off my shoes. "Here, hold these," I said as I passed my shoes to Dakota.

I ran out to meet the Maasai.

Nebala was leading. His mouth was wide open and there was sweat pouring off him. Koyati was next. He was a dozen paces back. His teeth were gritted and he looked as though he was working hard. Right tight behind him, no more than a step, was Samuel. He saw me, waved, and gave me a big smile.

I fell in beside Nebala. "How are you?"

"Tired," he panted.

"Yeah, of course. You're doing brilliantly. You've gained over a minute on the big group in second place."

"And . . . and . . . the men who are winning?" he asked.

I almost didn't want to answer, but I had no choice. "You're gaining on them . . . a little."

"How . . . little?"

"Less than thirty seconds—just run!"

He yelled something over his shoulder and then he started running even faster—too fast for me to keep up any longer. I came to an abrupt stop, and Koyati and Samuel brushed past me.

I moved over to the side and slowly walked back. Olivia, my mother, and Dakota were standing beside his golf cart. Then I noticed that there was only one cart. Where was our golf cart? And where was our driver? Had Dakota told him to leave as part of a plan to get us off the course? I'd show him a plan of my own when I drove off in his golf cart!

"Where is our cart?" I demanded.

"I sent it away," he said.

"You had no right to do that!"

"Of course I did. I'm the director of the race, remember? I can do pretty well whatever I want."

"You can't chase us away that easily!" I snapped.

"Nobody is trying to chase you anywhere."

"How are we supposed to get around without our cart?"

"This wonderful young man is going to be our guide for the rest of the marathon," my mother said, motioning to Dakota.

"*You're* going to drive us?" I asked in disbelief.

"It will be my honour. By the way . . . very nice shoes."

I'd forgotten that I was standing barefoot, and that he was holding my shoes.

"Very elegant . . . very stylish . . . Prada, of course."

"Yes, they are . . . and thank you."

He handed me the shoes and I slipped them on.

"Now, we should be going. Please . . . all aboard," he said as he bowed and gestured to the cart.

I hesitated for a second as my mother and Olivia climbed onto the back. There was no point in standing there. Reluctantly I climbed into the passenger seat as he climbed in behind the wheel, and we started up.

"These Maasai have been generating a great deal of coverage," he said.

"That's great, because I'd like to tell the press how you tried to keep them out of the race."

"Can you blame me?"

"Yes, actually, I do blame you. So what exactly changed your attitude?"

"The reaction of the crowds, the press coverage, and of course, the website that started it all. That is an amazing website you designed."

"Not me. My mother is the webmaster."

He looked slightly over his shoulder at her. "Brilliant work. The pictures, the video clips, flash, and the overall layout! It's so rare to find somebody with that combination of technical know-how and sense of style!"

"You are so kind."

"I know you're probably booked up so far in advance that you can't accommodate it, but I was wondering if you would consider coming on board and designing our site for next year."

"I think I might be able to find the time," my mother said.

"We'd make it very much worth your while."

"I'm sure we can discuss this further. Perhaps next week."

"Wonderful!" he exclaimed. "Do you have a business card so I can contact you?"

Business cards? There was no way she had business cards.

"Not with me, I'm afraid," my mother said. "I'll have my personal assistant contact you after the race."

Personal assistant? Business cards? Did she have a company jet that I didn't know about as well?

"I'm very interested in how you are going to portray what happens next on your website," Dakota said.

"What does that mean?" I asked.

"Well, it's such a wonderful story—selling their cattle, flying halfway around the world, and doing it all to raise money for the well for their community . . ."

"That's all on the website?" I asked.

"*You* haven't seen it?" he questioned, as if he couldn't believe his ears.

This was becoming a recurring, embarrassing theme. I should have looked, and it was now becoming increasingly painful that I hadn't.

"I've been very busy," I said, "training them for the run and everything." It was time to change the subject. "But getting back to my original question, what do you mean by 'what happens next'?"

"The part where they can't drill the well because they don't win the race."

"What makes you think they can't win?" I demanded.

"I think it's becoming obvious," Dakota said.

"Not obvious to me!" I protested.

"Look, don't get me wrong. I'd love for them to win."

"And that's why you put them in the back of the pack."

"That," he said, "was a major miscalculation on my part. If I had known then what a big story this was going to be they would have been right on the front line. But it's too late for that now. And, I'm afraid, too late for them to win."

"They still have lots of time."

He shook his head. "Not enough time, not enough distance. You know the numbers."

"I know the numbers, but you don't know the Maasai. They don't know how to quit."

"Quit, no. Collapse, yes. You saw them at the fifteen-mile mark."

"Of course I saw them. Your point being?"

"Then you saw how much they were struggling," he said.

"You must have been looking at the wrong Maasai."

"I appreciate your loyalty, but really . . . Look, they're not too far ahead. I'll pull alongside them and you can see for yourself."

I didn't want to say anything—I wasn't going to say anything—but I had noticed that Koyati did look as if he was struggling, and Samuel didn't seem to be able to keep up with Nebala either. Dakota pushed the little cart harder, and the electric engine whined louder.

"Did you notice the camera crew shadowing them?" Dakota asked.

"I did," Olivia said. "On the back of a motorcycle."

"That's right," Dakota said. "I pulled one of the cameras off the leaders and had him focus on them. I see that crew right up ahead."

There, not far in front of us, was a motorcycle carrying a cameraman on the back. He had his camera aimed at the runners—and there were Nebala, Koyati, and Samuel. As we closed in, the cheers of the crowd started to sound louder than the whining of the electric golf cart engine. We pulled up until we were just behind the motorcycle, paralleling them as they ran.

"They really are popular," Dakota said. "I just wish they could win."

"Why are you so certain they can't?"

"Just look," he said. "The leader . . . what's his name?"

"Nebala."

"He's struggling. Do you see his steps, how short and choppy they are?"

"He looks like he's doing just fine," I argued.

"Okay, fine. How about the second runner?"

Koyati was now two dozen paces behind Nebala.

"You have to admit that he's having some difficulties."

His head was down, but I could still see the strain on his face, and it looked as though he was favouring one leg—one stride was longer than the other.

"I don't know what's keeping him upright and going forward," Dakota said.

"The Maasai don't know how to quit."

"He may be a Maasai, but he certainly isn't a runner. Wrong body type, wrong stride."

I wanted to argue, but arguing wouldn't change the truth of what he had said. Koyati was running on nothing more than sheer determination.

"Now that third runner is a different matter," Dakota said.

"You mean Samuel . . . the one in the back?"

"I don't know why he is at the rear. He's a real runner. Look at him!"

I didn't know much about running and runners, but even I could see what he meant. Samuel was moving as

though it were effortless. He was gliding over the pavement, and there wasn't even any strain in his face. In
fact, he really reminded me of the runners who were
somewhere up at the front of the pack. He did run differently from Koyati, or even Nebala.

Samuel looked in our direction. He saw us, broke
into a big smile, and waved. He didn't look like he had
run over fifteen miles. He looked like he was just out
for a gentle stroll.

"Do you see what I mean?" Dakota asked. "I don't
know why he isn't running harder. Why isn't he in
front of the other two?"

Maybe Dakota didn't know—but I did.

CHAPTER TWENTY-FIVE

"Drive over beside them," I said to Dakota.

"I can't do that."

"Why not?"

"Insurance and liability. The support vehicles have to stay away from the runners."

"Forget liability. I need to speak to them, so you *have* to do it."

I reached over and grabbed the wheel and swerved the cart. Olivia shrieked, and Dakota snatched the wheel back, regaining control.

"What do you think you're doing?" he yelled.

"I have to talk to Nebala."

I reached for the wheel again, but he blocked my efforts.

"Just listen. I think I know why Samuel isn't running faster."

"You do?"

"Yes, and if I could talk to Nebala maybe I could take care of it, get Samuel to run faster . . . to have him maybe finish sooner . . . It would be a better story, wouldn't it?"

Dakota looked at me and then turned slightly over his shoulder. "Hang on, ladies."

He turned the cart and angled it toward the centre of the boulevard and the runners. There weren't that many runners, and they were pretty strung out. I wasn't sure why he was so worried about hitting somebody.

"I need to talk to Samuel and Koyati first."

He brought us in so we were right beside Koyati, with Samuel just a half step behind. Samuel flashed me a big smile. Koyati didn't react. It was as though he hadn't noticed we were there.

His eyes were on the ground in front of him, his mouth was open, and he was panting and puffing, struggling and straining to get his breath. It was like he had to focus all his energy on just putting one foot in front of the other. It was pretty obvious that, Maasai or no Maasai, there was no way he was going to be able to keep on running this fast for the next nine or ten miles. Not only was he not going to be able to gain on the leaders, but it was just a matter of time until— Just then he stumbled, almost tripping, recovered, and kept running!

"Koyati!" I yelled.

He turned his head slightly to see me. His eyes were glazed over. Ten miles was out of the question. Could he keep going another ten minutes?

"Are you okay?" I asked.

He gritted his teeth and gave me a slight nod. He was obviously not okay.

I turned to Samuel. "How about you?"

"Doing good, dude!" He put both thumbs up in the air. He looked as though he *was* doing pretty good—not like a guy in the middle of running a marathon, but like someone who was running to the corner store to pick up a loaf of bread.

"Samuel, can you run faster?"

"Yes, faster, yes."

"Then why *aren't* you running faster?" Dakota asked him.

Samuel shrugged.

"I know why," I told Dakota.

"You do?"

"Pretty sure. I need to talk to Nebala now."

Nebala was now quite a bit in front of the other two—fifty or sixty feet. Dakota brought us in right beside him.

Nebala was doing better than Koyati, but it was obvious he was struggling too. I could see the strain in his face, and his steps were now shorter and choppier.

"Nebala," I called out. "You cannot win unless you move faster!"

"Faster?" he gasped in disbelief.

"Much faster, but I don't think Koyati can move any faster, or for much longer." I paused. "I don't know if *you* can run faster." I paused again to see his reaction. He didn't argue, so he didn't disagree.

"But Samuel can run faster. You just have to give him permission to run faster . . . permission to pass Koyati and you."

I was positive that's what was holding him back. He couldn't pass Koyati because he was his elder, and Nebala was not only his elder, but also the king's son!

"Tell him it wouldn't be disrespectful if he passed you. That you *want* him to pass you."

Nebala didn't react. Had he heard me? Had he understood what I was asking, what it meant? He just kept looking forward, running—and then he broke stride and we rolled past him. I looked back at him—at them.

He had slowed enough for Koyati and Samuel to catch him, and then he fell in beside them. They were talking—well, Nebala was talking, and the other two were listening. Koyati stumbled, and Nebala reached out and grabbed him by the arm to steady him. There was more conversation, and then Samuel burst past the other two.

In long, fluid strides he picked up speed, quickly pulling away from his friends. Within seconds he had caught up to us. He flashed another smile.

"Run, Samuel! Run fast!"

I stood right beneath the big twenty-mile clock so I could keep one eye on the time and the other on the racers. The clock was just coming up to the 1:46:00 mark, and the first runners were in view . . . but there were only two of them now. Off to the side was a motorcycle carrying a cameraman. As they got closer the spectators reacted with cheers and applause.

The two runners were moving quickly, fluidly, easily. One was following the second so closely that it looked as if they were connected. They passed us as the clock ticked off 1:46:15.

I turned and looked back down the road, hoping beyond hope to see Samuel in third place. That wasn't reasonable, and I knew that. He'd been two and a half minutes behind at the fifteen-mile mark, and he hadn't kicked it into top gear until over a mile after that.

There was a stretch of open pavement and then a single runner. He was probably the runner who had been with the front runners through the fifteen-mile mark. And then, after another stretch of open pavement, was the pack. I couldn't tell how many runners were in that group, but it didn't look as big as it had.

"He might have hit the wall," Dakota said.

"He wouldn't hit any walls," I scoffed. "He isn't blind."

"The wall isn't a real wall," he said. "It's an *imaginary* wall."

"Like that explains it."

"It's a phenomenon marathon runners experience around the eighteenth or nineteenth mile," he explained. "They're running well and then—*bang*—they can't go any farther."

"There he is!" Olivia screamed.

I caught sight of him. He was well behind the pack but definitely within striking distance! If he'd hit any wall he'd broken right through it! He was moving quickly. It looked as though he was still gaining on the runners in front of him

A wave of applause overwhelmed us as the third runner came past: 1:46:45. He'd gained thirty seconds on the leaders since the fifteen-mile mark.

The applause faded for just a few seconds, and then a second wave of cheering started up. The pack was closing in, and Samuel was closing in on them! He was so close that he was almost part of the pack!

There was a wave of applause, screaming, yelling, cheering as the crowd standing around us responded to their approach. It was clearly louder and wilder than the cheering for the leaders.

The first member of the pack ran past us and the clock: 1:47:10. Almost immediately the next runner, and then two or three more, and then another cluster of five or six, and then—

"Hello, Alexandria! Hello, Olivia! Hello, Alexandria's mother!" Samuel yelled as he ran by, waving and smiling!

The crowd started cheering even more loudly, and then Samuel started blowing kisses! The crowd erupted, went totally wild, and surged out onto the boulevard as he passed!

CHAPTER TWENTY-SIX

"What a story!" Dakota exclaimed.

We drove along in the golf cart, right beside Samuel. He was now leading the pack, moving at an incredible pace, pulling them along with him and gaining on the leaders. They'd passed mile twenty-one, then twenty-two, and twenty-three, and twenty-four. They were less than thirty seconds behind the two leaders, but they had less than two miles to catch them. Samuel was now in fourth place—and fourth place was good for $75,000! That was almost enough to pay for everything—a well, airfare home, plus enough to buy back the cows they'd sold.

Part of me wanted to just yell that Samuel should take it easy, that he didn't have to win, but I knew I couldn't slow him down even if I wanted to. And who knew? Maybe he could win! That would mean enough money to buy ten wells and enough cows to make the three of them just about the richest Maasai in Africa!

All along the route the crowd was getting larger, deeper, and louder! The cheers were almost deafening. And as the crowd continued to grow, the boundary that separated spectators from runners, maintained only by that little rope, was becoming more blurred. Repeatedly Dakota had to slow down or steer around people who should have been on the sidewalk but were out on the road. He kept yelling into his walkie-talkie, demanding that more security, more police officers, and more officials come down to the lines to hold back the crowd. It wasn't working. The route for the runners—and the motorcycles and golf carts— was becoming narrower and narrower. If they didn't get the crowd back, I didn't know how the mass of runners taking up the rear would ever squeeze by.

I wondered how Nebala and Koyati were doing. We'd abandoned them to stay with Samuel.

"Can you radio back and tell me where Nebala and Koyati are?" I asked Dakota.

"Sure . . . hold on." He barked a couple of questions into his walkie-talkie, one of which was about my Maasai.

A burst of answers came back. They were now over a mile back and falling farther and farther off the pace. Koyati had practically broken down. He had "hit the wall" and was still struggling but moving very slowly.

Nebala had also slowed down to be with him. One of the reports said that he was actually "helping" him move forward, which meant, according to Dakota, that both runners were now officially disqualified from the race for "receiving assistance." Even if they did manage to get to the end they wouldn't officially have completed it.

That was sad but expected, and besides, even if they did finish it wasn't like they would be fast enough to qualify for any prize money. I could just picture them running, Nebala helping to keep Koyati up, with each step getting closer to the finish but farther from the front as more and more runners passed them by. But none of that mattered. All that mattered was Samuel.

He was now well clear of the pack—which had thinned to less than ten runners—and hot on the tail of the third-place runner. Up ahead of that runner were the two leaders. For the first time on this long straightaway section I could actually see Samuel *and* the leaders! Maybe winning wasn't impossible. If you had seen them then you would have had to believe it was possible. Seeing was believing. But first, he had to move up into third place.

"Can you get ahead of the front runners so we can be waiting at the twenty-five-mile mark?" I asked Dakota.

"Sure," he replied. "And then we want to get to the finish line. It's important to be there when the first runners cross the line."

"Do you think he has a chance to catch them?" I asked.

"I'm through making predictions. None of what he's done is possible."

He pushed down on the pedal of the little cart, and we picked up speed. Repeatedly he sounded the horn and steered around spectators who were spilling out and onto the road.

"Get off the road!" he yelled as he almost mowed down a group who had surged forward to have a look at the runners.

Then I realized that they were looking not forward at the leaders but back toward Samuel. As we closed in and caught up with the two leaders, I saw that the crowd seemed remarkably uninterested in them and were just waiting for Samuel to pass. The roar of the crowd was coming from *behind* us now.

Dakota pulled in right underneath the twenty-five-mile clock, and we all climbed out of the cart. My mother instantly pulled out her camera and started to take pictures. She snapped some shots as the first two runners raced toward us and then past. People cheered as they passed, but it was almost like they were doing it out of politeness. I looked at the clock: 2:05:03.

I turned to look back for Samuel. There he was, not far behind the third-place runner. He was charging along the straightaway and he was gaining, and gaining quickly. The crowd started cheering, screaming at the top of their lungs. Samuel was going to pass him and take over third place! The crowd could see what was going to happen, but the runner in front of Samuel had no idea.

Then he looked over his shoulder and saw Samuel. He seemed startled and then started running faster—much faster. He started to pull away from Samuel, quickly opening up some pavement between them. Samuel reacted and began to run faster too, closing the gap as quickly as it had opened. The crowd was practically going insane!

The runner looked over his left shoulder as Samuel came up on his right side. Samuel pulled even and got a half step ahead before the other runner realized where he was and accelerated even more. The two men were now matching each other, side by side, stride by stride. They were practically sprinting along— and they slammed into a man who had stepped out of the crowd! All three of them went tumbling head over heels, rolling and skidding along the pavement!

CHAPTER TWENTY-SEVEN

The whole crowd, every single person, seemed to stop cheering all at once. There was silence, and then a loud, collective gasp.

The three men were in a heap, and there was a mess of arms and legs and body parts all tangled together. They rolled away from one another and became three separate men again. The other runner, his left leg all scraped and bleeding, staggered to his feet and started to run. Samuel got to his knees. He looked shocked, surprised, hurt . . . He looked as though he was in pain.

"Samuel!" I screamed. "Get up!"

He snapped back to reality. He got to his feet and practically fell over again, stumbling as he tried to run! He took a step forward, but when he tried to put down the second foot it collapsed under him and he fell to the pavement! The entire crowd fell completely silent again, holding their breath, waiting, watching, in shock.

I ran out to where he had fallen. My mother and Olivia and Dakota were right behind me. I reached out to offer him my hand and—

"Don't touch him!" Dakota yelled. "If you offer him assistance he's disqualified!"

I drew back my hand. "Samuel, are you all right?" I asked, although obviously he wasn't.

"Foot . . . foot," he said. He had rolled over to sit on the pavement, and he was clutching his left ankle with both hands.

"Let me see it," my mother said. "Move your hands away."

Reluctantly he removed his hands. I didn't need to wait for my mother's opinion. His ankle was already starting to swell.

"It's sprained," my mother said. "Badly sprained."

"That's it . . . the race is over . . . He can't run an—"

"No!" Samuel yelled. "Not over . . . not over."

He struggled to his feet—or more correctly, his foot. He held the injured foot off the ground.

"You can't go any farther," my mother said.

"There's no point in going any farther," Dakota said. "Your race is over."

As if to prove the truth of his words, the pack of runners—eight or nine of them—ran around us.

"You can't possibly catch them. You can't win on one leg," Dakota said. "Let me call for a stretcher so you can have your ankle—"

Samuel shook his head vigorously. "Run."

"But you can't win."

Samuel shrugged. "Run."

He took a step on his bad foot and grimaced in pain but hopped forward onto his good foot. He took another short step and then hopped onto his good foot.

"This is insane!" Dakota said. "There are liability issues! I've got to stop him before . . ."

His words were drowned out by the crowd. They began to clap and cheer and scream. All of them, even those who had been sitting on the curb, were now on their feet cheering. We stood there and watched as Samuel limped forward. He wasn't able to move any faster than a slow, painful-looking walk, more a hop than anything resembling a run. But he was moving, and as he moved the crowd reaction rippled forward with him. It was unbelievable, much louder than anything I'd ever heard before.

I put my mouth close to Dakota's ear so I could be heard. "If you try to take him out of race the crowd will kill you."

He nodded his head. "I won't do that . . . but not because of the crowd. He deserves to try to finish. We need to stay close to watch him."

"Can I stay with him? Can I run beside him?"

"Normally we can't allow a non-participant on the course . . . but . . . but just go . . . Be with him."

"Thank you so much!" I trotted forward on my heels. There was no need to take them off to keep up with him.

I ran to his side. He turned his head slightly to face me.

"Samuel, I'm going to stay with you."

He tried to smile through gritted teeth. He kept on moving. Each time he put that foot down I could see his body react as the pain radiated up his leg. I could almost feel the pain myself. I had to fight the urge to help him.

The crowd continued to roar its approval, and I got the feeling that they were helping him to keep moving forward.

Four runners—two on one side and two on the other—swooshed past us. I couldn't help counting— he was now somewhere between fifteenth and twentieth. If somehow nobody else passed he'd still win some— Oh, that was just stupid.

I looked back at the course. There were another dozen runners visible along the long, straight section of pavement. All of them would pass in the next thirty seconds, and probably another dozen after that, and another dozen, until he ended up in five hundredth place. But I knew he couldn't stop. He was Maasai. He couldn't win, but he wouldn't quit.

We passed the twenty-six-mile mark. I didn't even want to look at the clock, but I couldn't stop myself: 3:02:25. The winner had completed the race almost an hour ago. Hundreds of runners had finished. Hundreds and hundreds and hundreds. I'd lost track some time back of the runners whizzing past us.

I'd seen most of those runners twice. Once when they'd passed us and a second time after they'd finished and had come back to cheer us on. Hundreds of runners had walked or run back and cheered just as loudly as the spectators. The roar of the crowd had continued to grow. There were race cameras trained on us, but also the local television stations had heard and had sent their cameras. Along with them were the thousands of people with their own cameras. We'd had enough shots taken of us in the last hour to make a supermodel jealous. I just wished I'd worn something different, and all this walking and running had done absolutely nothing for my makeup. I had sweated . . . perspired . . . *glowed* more than I would have liked.

Of course it wasn't me they were interested in. If I'd just walked away nobody would have been taking *any* pictures of me.

"It isn't much farther," I said to Samuel.

He nodded.

"Less than three hundred yards. Look up and you can see the finish."

He took his eyes from the ground and looked ahead. The banner over the finish line was clearly visible. He was going to make it.

The cheering of the crowd suddenly got, impossibly, even louder. Why now? I looked behind us— there were Nebala and Koyati. They'd kept going and they'd caught up to us!

They weren't running very fast—it was obvious that Koyati was struggling badly—but they were still moving much faster than us. Everybody was moving faster than us. They came up beside us, one on each side, and then slowed down so they matched our pace.

Samuel said something to Nebala. I didn't understand the words, but I understood the tone. He was apologizing. Nebala responded by saying a few words, nodding his head, and putting a hand on Samuel's shoulder. He was telling him that it was okay . . . that he understood . . . that he forgave him.

The four of us moved forward. It was right that the three of them were going to finish together. But it wasn't right for me to be with them. I wasn't a participant, and Samuel didn't need me anymore. He had them.

I stopped running and let them move forward without me. That would put the focus where it belonged, on them. Besides, it gave me a minute or so out of the spotlight. I knew that Olivia had a hairbrush in her purse, and I had my makeup in mine . . . I could do a little touch-up. There would definitely be photographers at the end, and I wanted to look my best for those shots.

I moved off the course to the side and continued to walk as the three of them limped toward the finish line. They hadn't won the race. They hadn't won any prize money. There wouldn't be any money for the well, or to buy cows, or even to buy airplane tickets. How were they going to get home? I wasn't too worried about that, though—I knew I could talk to my father. He'd be able to take care of it.

The cheering got louder as the three approached the finish line. They crossed the line and then they disappeared as they were engulfed in a crowd of runners and spectators. When they reappeared, they were lifted up high above the crowd, carried on people's shoulders!

They hadn't won the race, but they hadn't quit. They *were* Maasai.

CHAPTER TWENTY-EIGHT

It was three hours since the winners had crossed the finish line—two hours since the Maasai had completed the race—and only in the last fifteen minutes had the crowd started to drift away. Every runner, every spectator, dozens of reporters and television crews—where had they all come from?—they all wanted to talk to, interview, congratulate, back-slap, or take a picture of Nebala, Koyati, and Samuel, in particular.

There was so much attention on the three of them that the winner had all but been ignored. I felt sorry for him. At least, as sorry I could be for somebody who'd just won $250,000.

I really felt sorry for—well, bad for—my Maasai. Though they stood there stoically, this all had to be so painful for them. They had said they were going to win the money and return to build a well. They had lost, and they had no money, so there wasn't going to be a well. For them, not winning was like not keeping their word, and a Maasai always kept his word. I wondered how hard it would be for them to return to their village.

And then, even worse, they were being asked to relive their loss—their dishonour—in interview after interview. One crew even showed them replays—Nebala and Koyati struggling and being passed by runner after runner, Samuel falling and then hobbling forward, the three of them crossing the finish line—and asked them for their comments, their *"feelings,"* about what had happened.

I knew they had feelings—terrible feelings of hurt—but they would never reveal those feelings. I think the interviewer wanted some kind of emotional outburst. Instead, they were calm, showing no emotion. The interviewer didn't know that you couldn't get an emotional outburst from a Maasai if you broke his arm. I knew that. I also knew that they must be in pain . . . Samuel because of his ankle, but all of them because they'd failed.

This interviewer—he was from Channel Nine News—wasn't talking to them as much as using them as background. I'd seen him on the news before. He was a pretty-boy with great clothes and better hair. He looked like he lived in *The Hills*.

"I stand with three brave Maasai," the reporter said, gesturing to Nebala, Koyati, and Samuel standing beside him. "They came to Beverly Hills to run in the marathon. They tried to win a race, not for personal gain, and not for glory, but simply to raise funds to build a well for their destitute community ... a well that would have been used to water crops, for livestock, and simply for drinking water. They came with this simple and noble dream." He paused and looked directly into the camera. "A dream that lies shattered on twenty-six miles of pavement." He paused, and I looked for a reaction from Nebala— there was none. "This is Bart Stone, reporting live from Beverly Hills."

The bright lights faded. "That's a wrap," the man behind the camera called out.

Good old Bart shook hands with the Maasai, and he and his camera crew quickly departed.

"Excuse me, but that's a wrap for *everybody!*" Dakota called out. "They've given enough interviews."

There was grumbling and some groans from those still waiting for their turn.

"Come on, people, have some understanding. These men have just run a marathon—him on one foot," he said, pointing at Samuel. "They need to rest." He turned to me. "Let's all go to my office, where we can talk in private."

I didn't really have anything to talk about, but I was happy to get away from the crowd. I'd never thought I would get tired of having my picture taken, but this was too much. I had no idea how *anybody* could ever get used to this. It had to be incredibly draining on the rich and famous and beautiful to have to deal with this all the time. I didn't know if I could face that. If that was to become my fate ... well, I figured

I could always hire enough big, burly security people to keep the paparazzi at a safe distance.

Dakota shepherded us toward his office. I hung behind at the back of the line so I could speak to my father.

"Did you get them?" I asked.

He nodded.

"When?"

"Two weeks from now."

"Nothing sooner?"

"I'm afraid not. Is that going to be a problem?"

"No, of course not."

We walked into the office and Dakota closed the door, sealing us off from the crush of press and well-wishers. It got a lot quieter.

"Please, everybody take a seat," he said.

The three Maasai and Olivia sat down together on the big leather chesterfield. My mother came over and brought a chair. She lifted up Samuel's ankle—which the medics had checked out at the scene and encased with ice—and carefully placed his foot on the chair. Samuel grimaced ever so slightly and gritted his teeth, trying to resist reacting to the pain he must have been feeling. His ankle was a swollen mess. It was a very bad sprain, but apparently all it needed was rest.

"This has certainly been an incredible end to an incredible day," Dakota said. He got up from his desk and stood right in front of Nebala. "And I speak for all of us when I say how proud we are of your efforts."

Nebala looked up. "I do not understand. There is nothing to be proud of."

"Of course there is! You three are heroes!"

Nebala scoffed. "Heroes win. We failed."

"I don't think that's how anybody sees it."

"We did not win."

There wasn't much to argue with. I didn't see them as failures either, but they hadn't won, and as far as they were concerned that was all that mattered.

"Look, the only reason you didn't win was because of me," Dakota said. "If I'd placed you in a better position none of this would have happened. *You* didn't fail . . . *I* didn't allow you to succeed."

Wow, I didn't see that coming. I guess a guy who knew Prada had to have some class, and he was showing it.

"And that's why I want to extend an invitation to you to participate in next year's marathon."

"You want them to come back?" Olivia questioned.

"Not only come back, but I will guarantee them a starting spot on the first line, and they will receive an appearance fee."

"An appearance fee?" my father asked. "How much are we talking about?"

"Well, I can't give an exact figure at this point, but I can guarantee it will be sufficient to cover airfare, hotel, and a small sum on top of that."

"If you want them back it's going to have to be more than a *small* sum," my father said.

Dakota smiled. "We can certainly enter into negotiations."

"Judging from the reaction of the crowd and the media, I would think it would be in your best interests to be very generous in those negotiations." My father smiled. "Unless, of course, you want to see them compete in the New York or Boston marathon instead."

"No, no! I don't think that will be necessary. We take care of our runners. I give you my word that it will be a very generous offer." He paused. "Do we have a deal?"

My father got up, extended his hand to shake, and—

"Wait!" I said, stepping between them. "I think we have to ask Nebala what they want to do."

"Of course . . . excuse me!" My father looked genuinely embarrassed. He never missed a chance to make a lucrative deal, but he was forgetting whose decision this was.

I put my hand on Nebala's shoulder and he looked up. "Do you want to come back and run next year?"

"Next year? I . . . I cannot say what will happen next year . . . I do not know."

"I understand," I said. "You need time to think about everything that has happened, time just to go home and—"

"We cannot go home."

We all knew that they didn't have return tickets or the money to buy tickets. But I knew they *could* go home. I looked at my father, and we exchanged little smiles.

"Why don't you tell them?" I said to my father.

He shook his head. "It was your idea. You should tell them."

That was nice of him.

"You *can* go home. My father got you airline tickets."

"That's one of the things I was doing while everybody else was giving interviews and being TV stars," my father said. "You'll be leaving in—"

"We have no money to pay," Nebala said, cutting him off.

"No, no, you don't have to pay!" I said. "The tickets are a gift."

"Your family has given us so much already. We are grateful, but we cannot accept your tickets," Nebala said.

"I've already bought the tickets," my father said. "If you don't take them, they'll just go to waste."

"My father's right. Besides, if you don't take the tickets, how will you get home?" I asked.

"We will not get home. We cannot go home."

"What do you mean?"

"We have failed. We are too . . . too . . . There is too much . . . shame."

I looked at my father. He always had an answer to everything.

"Daddy?"

"What if I were to give you the money for the well? Then you could go home."

"You are a kind and generous man, but we cannot take your money."

My father shrugged his shoulders. This time there was no answer.

"Then what are you going to do?" I asked. "Where are you going to go?"

"We will go as soon as Samuel has healed."

"Go where? Where will you go?"

Nebala shrugged. "We will walk."

This was insane! Did they think they could walk back to Africa? Or were they just going to wander around the States?

"Look, there has to be another way," I said. "Dakota, can you give them some appearance money for participating in this year's marathon?"

"I wish I could, but there's nothing left in the budget. I'm so sorry."

There had to be an answer. There was always an answer. I just had to think harder and I knew I could come up with—

"What about Hollywood Boulevard?" Olivia suggested.

"What *about* Hollywood Boulevard?" I asked.

"We can take them back to Hollywood Boulevard, and they can pose for pictures for the tourists."

"Olivia, you're a genius!" I exclaimed. "That could work!"

"They can't earn that much money posing for pictures, can they?" my father asked.

"They might be able to earn three or four hundred dollars a day," Olivia said.

"And how much is it that they need?" my father asked.

"With everything . . . maybe fifty or sixty thousand dollars."

"So it would take them quite a long time to earn that much," my father said.

"At three or four hundred dollars a day, it would be between one hundred and twenty-five and one hundred and seventy-seven days, assuming they need only fifty thousand dollars, but if it's sixty thousand, then it would take—"

"A very long time," my father said, cutting me off.

"Maybe none of that will be necessary," my mother said.

I looked over. She was sitting at Dakota's desk and her eyes were on his computer screen. What was she doing? And was she going to finish that thought?

"Mom?"

"You should have a look at the website I built."

"I will, and I'm really sorry I didn't look before— that was wrong—but I don't think this is the time," I said. "We have to find a solution."

"I *have* a solution. You all should come and see this. Please."

Everybody got to their feet and we crowded around my mother, looking at the screen. There were pictures—wonderful pictures of Nebala and Samuel and Koyati. And there was text explaining why they were here and what they were going to do with the money. It was a great site, but how was this a solution to the problem?

"I put a couple of things on the site . . . I had to, for my assignment. I needed to know how many people had visited the site, so I put a counter on the page."

I looked where she had pointed. "Is that right? There have been over one hundred thousand hits . . . in four days?" I gasped.

"Three days, and yes, that number is correct. That's the power of the Internet. But here's the really important part."

She clicked on another page and then scrolled down to the bottom.

"I put a link on the page so people could make contributions to a bank account I set up," she said.

"You mean, like, donate money?"

"Money and other things," she said. "Look at this e-mail. It's from the president of Kenya Airways, and he's donated three first-class tickets for them to return home."

"That's incredible! But . . . but they still don't have money for the well," I said. I knew that their pride wouldn't allow them to return empty-handed, even if they had a way to get there.

"That isn't going to be a problem either," my mother said. "People have also been donating money. And so far, this is how much has been contributed."

She pointed to the screen. There was a collective gasp from me, Olivia, and my father.

"Eighty-three thousand dollars? There's eighty-three thousand dollars?" I couldn't believe my eyes.

"As of this moment, but there's going to be more, I'm sure," my mother said. "It will keep on accumulating."

"That's incredible!" I exclaimed. "That's enough money to build a well, buy back your cattle, and still have lots left over!"

I wrapped my arms around my mother.

"There are people who are giving us money?" Nebala asked.

"Lots and lots of people," my mother said. "Many are giving only a little, five or ten or twenty dollars, but it all adds up."

"But why?" Nebala asked. "Why are they doing this?"

"Because they want to help," my mother said.

This was wonderful, but I could instantly see a problem, an objection Nebala was going to make. Would he see this as any different from my father giving them money?

"We cannot take this—"

"Yes, you can!" I said, cutting Nebala off before he could finish his sentence. "And the reason you can is because you *earned* the money." I took a deep breath so I could think. This had to be perfect. "They all saw that you didn't win the race, but they know that you didn't *lose*, because you refused to quit."

Nebala shrugged. "We are Maasai. We could not quit."

"And you showed them how to keep going, even when they feel like quitting. You've taught them all a lesson. You've taught them about courage, about determination, about what it is to be a Maasai—and that's why you earned the money. You were all like teachers . . . and teachers get paid, don't they?"

He gave a little shrug. He wasn't sure I was right, but he wasn't sure I wasn't.

"And that's why you can't quit now. You have to take the money back and build the well. Not just for you, but for everybody in your community." I paused. "You came here not to win the race but to get enough money to build that well. You did it, and I'm proud of you."

I turned to my mother. "And proud of you."

She smiled.

"Well?" I asked Nebala.

Everybody looked at him. Whatever he said would be the final word.

He slowly nodded his head. "We are going home," he said quietly.

Everybody screamed and cheered. Even Koyati broke into a big grin, and Samuel smiled broadly in spite of the pain.

"Hold on!" my father yelled, and everybody became quiet. "That leaves me with one slight problem. I have three tickets for Kenya that still need to used."

"When are they for?" my mother asked.

"Two weeks from now."

"And isn't March Break in two weeks?" she asked.

"Yeah, we're on a break from school . . . You don't mean . . . ?"

My mother pointed at Olivia, me, and herself. "One, two, three."

I looked at my father. "Daddy, would that be all right?"

"I don't see why not. They're already paid for."

I smiled. "It would be great to see Ruth, and of course, little Alexandria."

"And they would be glad to see you," Nebala said, smiling. "Look out, Kenya! Once again there will be two Alexandrias of Africa."